A DELUXE BOOK OF FLOWER FAIRIES™

A DELUXE BOOK OF FLOWER FAIRIES™

CICELY MARY
BARKER

FREDERICK WARNE

The material in this volume was originally published in four separate books:

FLOWER FAIRIES OF THE SPRING – A CELEBRATION
FLOWER FAIRIES OF THE SUMMER – A CELEBRATION
FLOWER FAIRIES OF THE AUTUMN – A CELEBRATION
FLOWER FAIRIES OF THE WINTER – A CELEBRATION

FREDERICK WARNE

Published by the Penguin Group
Penguin Books Ltd, 80 Strand, London WC2R 0RL, England
Penguin Putnam Inc., 375 Hudson Street, New York, New York 10014, USA
Penguin Books Australia Ltd, 250 Camberwell Road, Camberwell, Victoria 3124, Australia
Penguin Books Canada Ltd, 10 Alcorn Avenue, Toronto, Ontario, Canada M4V 3B2
Penguin Books India (P) Ltd, 11 Community Centre, Panchsheel Park, New Delhi 110 017, India
Penguin Books (NZ) Ltd, Cnr Rosedale and Airborne Roads, Albany, Auckland, New Zealand
Penguin Books (South Africa) (Pty) Ltd, P O Box 9, Parklands 2121, South Africa
Penguin Books Ltd, Registered Offices: 80 Strand, London WC2R 0RL, England
Web site at: www.flowerfairies.com

First published in four separate volumes by Frederick Warne 1998, 2000, 2001, 2002
This edition first published 2003
1 3 5 7 9 10 8 6 4 2
This edition copyright © Frederick Warne & Co., 2003
Text copyright © Frederick Warne & Co., 1998, 2000, 2001, 2002
New reproductions of Cicely Mary Barker's illustrations copyright © The Estate of Cicely Mary Barker, 1990
Original text and illustrations copyright © The Estate of Cicely Mary Barker, 1923, 1925, 1926,
1934, 1940, 1944, 1948, 2001

ISBN 0 7232 4939 3

Text for *Summer*, *Autumn* and *Winter* sections by Anna Trenter
Photographs and illustrations reproduced by kind permission of A–Z Botanical Collection Ltd,
Martin Barker, W. Broadhurst, Joan Dear, Garden Picture Library, Geoffrey Oswald, Anne Poole

Printed and bound in Singapore

~ Contents ~

~ Cicely Mary Barker ~

Cicely Mary Barker lived most of her life in Croydon, South London, but her imagination and artistry enabled her to envisage an invisible world that extended far beyond suburban Surrey. This magical realm, populated by fairies, was captured in her delightful poems and delicate drawings. Though she lived a quiet, modest life, Cicely Mary Barker achieved commercial success and world-wide renown with her Flower Fairies books. Today the public remains as enchanted with her creations as it was 75 years ago, when *Flower Fairies of the Spring* was first published.

Born on 28th June 1895 in Croydon, Cicely Mary Barker was the second child of Mary and Walter Barker. A frail child who suffered from epilepsy, Cicely was sheltered from the outside world by her parents and her older sister, Dorothy. The Barkers were a comfortable middle class family and they employed a nanny to educate Cicely at home and a cook to prepare her special meals. Despite her ill-health, Cicely enjoyed a happy, secure childhood and entertained herself with books and drawing.

Cicely's talent, evident from an early age, flourished quickly with the encouragement of her family and friends. Walter Barker, a partner in a seed supply company, was a capable watercolourist and he nurtured his youngest daughter's talent for drawing. When the family went on holiday, Cicely and her devoted father would sketch together by the seaside. Cicely's father enrolled her in a correspondence course for art tuition in 1908. That same year, aged only 13 years old, Cicely exhibited her work at the Croydon Art Society. In 1911, Cicely's father sold four of her drawings to the printer Raphael Tuck. Cicely also won second prize in the Croydon Art Society poster design competition and was elected a life member of the society. At 16 years old, Cicely was well on the way to a highly successful career.

*Cicely Mary Barker
as a young woman*

Unfortunately, Walter Barker did not live long enough to witness his daughter's rise to fame. He died in 1912 from a virus at the age of 43. His family sought comfort in their Christian faith but faced tightened economic circumstances. Dorothy, the more serious and practical of the two sisters, assumed the role of breadwinner. Having trained as a teacher, she began to teach a kindergarten class. Dorothy's salary enabled Cicely to continue drawing and pursuing her artistic goals.

Cicely contributed to the household finances by selling her poems and artwork to magazines such as *Child's Own, My Magazine* and Raphael Tuck annuals. She won a competition in 1914 sponsored by *The Challenge* magazine for her 'portrait of the editor as I imagine him to be'. Her early commercial work also included several series of watercolour postcards. The patriotic themes of the *Shakespeare's Children* and *Picturesque Children of the Allies* series proved very popular during the First World War. A charming precursor of her later work, Cicely's set of six *Fairy Cards* was commissioned by the S. Harvey Fine Art Publishing Co.

Between 1917 and 1918, Cicely embarked on the project that was to be her most famous. The Flower Fairies illustrations beautifully merged two of her favourite subjects – children and nature. Influenced by the Pre-Raphaelite artists, Cicely adhered to their practice of painting directly from nature. Cicely made numerous sketches of flowers to ensure that her drawings were botanically accurate and used local children as models. Gladys Tidy, the girl who did the Barkers' housework, sat for the Primrose Fairy. Wearing costumes made by Cicely, the young models posed holding the flower they were representing. Cicely's paintings skilfully convey the children's personalities as well as the flowers' appearances.

It was not until 1923 that Cicely searched for a publisher for *Flower Fairies of the Spring*. Although she received several rejections, Blackie accepted the work and paid her £25 for the 24 poems and paintings. The book was an instant success. In the first edition copies of *Flower Fairies of the Spring* that she presented to her mother and sister, Cicely inscribed sentimental poems expressing her gratitude for their support. The poem dedicated to Dorothy not only demonstrates respect and affection, but also reveals Cicely's concern about the effects of industrialization on the countryside.

Cicely Mary Barker (left) with her mother and sister Dorothy

> *To DOB*
> *By hedge and footpath, Hills and Hurst,*
> *Ere modern change had wrought its worst,*
> *Went you and I on Saturdays,*
> *And learnt the flowers and their ways.*
> *To you, best Teacher, do I owe*
> *The seed from which these fairies grow;*
> *Take then this Little Book the First*
> *Sprung from old lanes and fields and Hurst.*

An unworldly character, Cicely remained protected by her family from the outside world in adult life. It was her mother, for example, who wrote to Blackie before the publication of *Flower Fairies of the Summer* to ensure that Cicely received royalties for her work. As a result of being babied, Cicely retained a certain innocence and simplicity evident in her poetry.

The three Barker women moved to a smaller house in Croydon in 1924, where Dorothy established her own kindergarten and Cicely built a studio in the garden. Using her sister's pupils for inspiration and as models, Cicely continued her work on the Flower Fairies, producing a total of seven books for Blackie. Today, however, there are eight Flower Fairies titles in print. In 1985, Cicely's publishers compiled the volume *Flower Fairies of the Winter* from existing works, so there is now a book for every season.

The Flower Fairies were not Cicely's only work during the twenties, thirties, and forties. Blackie commissioned her to illustrate the covers of their *New Nursery Series* story books. Cicely wrote and illustrated two classic tales of her own, *The Lord of the Rushie River* and *Groundsel and Necklaces*, and illustrated several collections of rhymes. In addition to her children's illustrations, Cicely painted many religious pictures during this period. Both Cicely and Dorothy Barker were Sunday school teachers and regular church-goers. A collaboration between the sisters produced a book of Bible stories entitled *He Leadeth Me*. Cicely also began painting church panels and altar pieces in 1929. Like the Pre-Raphaelite artists, Cicely used ordinary parishioners as models for her devotional works, such as *The Parable of the Great Supper* which hangs in St. George's Church, Waddon.

Cicely Mary Barker on holiday

The Flower Fairies brought Cicely into contact with a fellow artist, Margaret Tarrant, who had painted her own versions of nature fairies. Though their styles were very different—Margaret's sprites were far more elfin and stylized than Cicely's naturalistic fairies—the two artists became close friends. They went on many sketching holidays together in Cornwall and along the South Coast. One of their favourite holiday destinations was Storrington in Sussex, where an artists' colony thrived.

Cicely Mary Barker
in later life

Though Cicely was perhaps closer to her artist friends than to her sister, Dorothy was sadly missed when she died of a heart attack in 1954. After her sister's death, Cicely undertook responsibility for housekeeping and caring for her elderly mother. This left little time for painting and her commercial career came to a halt. The fifties were a sad decade for Cicely and saw the death of many close friends and her beloved aunt, Head Deaconess Alice Oswald. When her mother died in 1960, Cicely moved from Croydon to Sussex.

Cicely's friend Edith Major had passed away and left her a cottage near Storrington. The house proved impractical for an elderly woman, but Cicely leased a maisonette in Storrington which she named St. Andrews, after her local church in Croydon. Despite her failing eyesight and weakening body, Cicely remained the active vice-president of the Croydon Art Society between 1961 and 1972. On 16th February 1973, after several prolonged stays in nursing homes, Cicely died at the age of 77.

In her obituaries, Cicely Mary Barker was remembered for her kindness, sense of humour and Christian faith, as well as her prodigious artistic talent. Her ashes were scattered in a glade in Storrington churchyard, where she could remain close to the Sussex countryside that she so dearly loved. Cicely Mary Barker's spirit endures in her Flower Fairies, which still delight new generations of children and admirers 75 years after they first appeared.

~ A Fairy History ~

Fairies enjoyed a surge of popularity in the mid 19th century. Fanciful stories and fairy tales were deemed frivolous in the 18th century, but Victorian writers and artists embraced the genre as an artistic antidote to the Industrial Revolution. Whereas earlier children's literature existed only to educate, the Victorians wrote books to amuse children. A Liberal Member of Parliament, Edward H. Knatchbull-Hugessen wrote fairy tales as a pastime. In 1886, he defended the need for entertaining children's literature in *Friends and Foes from Fairy Land*:

> To my mind there is enough of dry, prosy matter stuffed into their
> poor brains in these dull times, and a little lighter food is as
> useful as it is welcome to them.

Eminent writers such as John Ruskin used fairy tales to describe an idyllic world, far removed from repressive, utilitarian society. Publishers such as Raphael Tuck made fairy tales an affordable mass-market commodity. Born at the end of a century that is often called the golden age of children's literature, Cicely Mary Barker owned books by Kate Greenaway and Randolph Caldecott as a child and her artwork recalls certain elements of their illustrations.

*Cicely Mary Barker's
childhood books*

The passion for pixies continued into the early 20th century. In the years prior to the First World War, technology developed at a rapid pace. Electricity precipitated the invention of the wireless, the telephone, and the gramophone. This period also witnessed the spread of motor cars and the introduction of aeroplanes. Anxiety about the

In 'Picturesque Children of the Allies', Cicely painted children wearing traditional costumes against their nation's flag. These cards, published in 1915, appealed to nationalist sentiment.

damaging effects of these innovations was prevalent. Fairies, usually depicted in natural settings, represented a utopian alternative to modern life. Cicely, writing to a friend in 1923 after *Flower Fairies of the Spring* was published, lamented the disappearance of the countryside due to industrialization:

> There is no Cold Harbour Lane now, factories along Beddington Road; houses
> at the top of Russell Hill, and a Relief Road across it; fields chopped up;
> little streams drained away.

The success of the early Flower Fairies books, published after the destruction and carnage of the First World War, reveals the public's deep need for escapism through fancy. Similarly, the later Flower Fairies titles served to counter feelings of World War II gloom and malaise in the forties.

Cicely made frequent sketching trips to Sussex in the early forties to escape the damage of heavily bombed Croydon.

London hosted numerous avant garde exhibitions during the early 20th century, but Cicely was not influenced by the Cubist, Futurist or Surrealist movements of her day. Cicely's choice of subject may have been in vogue, but her style harks back to the Pre-Raphaelite artists who painted in the mid 19th century. These artists, led by Dante Gabriel Rossetti, William Holman Hunt and John Everett Millais, rejected chiaroscuro and art since the time of Raphael. Painting vibrant colours on white backgrounds, the Pre-Raphaelites called for 'truth to nature'. In 1899, the Barker family acquired a copy of *The Life and Letters of Sir John Everett Millais*. Cicely also admired Edward Burne-Jones and received the *Memorials of Edward Burne-Jones* as a Christmas present in 1920. Although some reviewers deemed her work outmoded, Cicely's Flower Fairies have stood the test of time and will continue to bring pleasure well into the 21st century.

A first edition cover printed in 1923

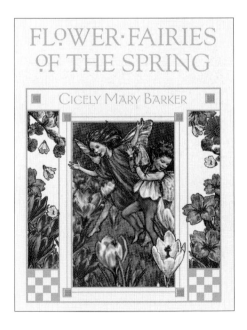

A recent cover, first printed in 2002

Throughout history, fairies have enjoyed popularity in times of economic depression or political strife. When humanity is at its emotional lowest, people look to the unknown to discover joy and magic. In the twenties, British illustrators such as Cicely, Margaret Tarrant, and Arthur Rackham painted whimsical pictures to brighten the spirits of their despairing post-war contemporaries. Though fairies eventually went out of fashion, they are currently experiencing a resurgence of popularity. The prominence of the New Age movement, emphasising nature and the Earth, has sparked a new interest in nature sprites, or fairies. Fairy shops, art exhibitions, and films about fairies all appeared in the nineties, a decade that also produced an economic recession. With the millennium approaching and society increasingly dominated by computers, fairies represented a return to innocence and nature. Having fascinated humans since the Middle Ages, the fairy world will always serve an important role in culture. They may be invisible, but fairies are here to stay.

A selection of modern Flower Fairies merchandise

~ A Fairy Time Line ~

1846 Hans Christian Andersen's *Wonderful Stories for Children* arrived in England.

1848 Pre-Raphaelite Brotherhood formed. Members included Dante Gabriel Rossetti, John Everett Millais, William Holman Hunt and later, Edward Burne-Jones.

1862 Christina Rossetti's *Goblin Market* published. This fairy poem was a favourite of Cicely's.

1864 Richard Dadd, the insane painter, finished his fairy masterpiece *The Fairy Feller's Master-Stroke* in Bedlam Hospital.

1865 Lewis Carroll's *Alice's Adventures in Wonderland* published.

1878 Kate Greenaway's *Under the Window* published.

1888 Oscar Wilde's *The Happy Prince* published.

1895 Cicely Mary Barker born in Croydon, South London.

1898 Edward Burne-Jones, Pre-Raphaelite artist, died.

1901 Queen Victoria died and Edward VII crowned king.

1904 *Peter Pan* opened at the Duke of York's theatre in London to popular acclaim.

1905 Motor buses introduced in London, one year before the London Underground opened. Taxis had appeared in London the previous year.

1906 J. M. Barrie's *Peter Pan in Kensington Gardens* published, illustrated by Arthur Rackham. Cicely was given a copy of the book in 1908.

1910 King Edward VII died and George V acceded the throne.
Rewards and Fairies, Rudyard Kipling's stories about Puck, published.

1911 Cicely Mary Barker sold four artworks to Raphael Tuck, printer of story books and annuals.

1914 Britain declared war on Germany, beginning World War I. New military inventions cause unprecedented destruction.

1915 *Princess Mary's Gift Book* published, featuring fairy poems by Alfred Noyes.

1916 Arthur Rackham illustrated *The Allies Fairy Book*.

1917 Elsie Wright, aged 17, and her cousin Frances Griffiths, aged 9, claimed to have photographed fairies in Cottingley, Yorkshire.

1918 Germany surrendered to the Allied forces on 11th November, ending four years of global conflict.

1922 Arthur Conan Doyle published *The Coming of the Fairies*. Margaret Tarrant painted *Do You Believe in Fairies?*

1923 *Flower Fairies of the Spring* published.

1925 *Flower Fairies of the Summer* published.

1926 *Flower Fairies of the Autumn* published.

1929 *Peter Pan* ended its West End run. Cicely wrote a poem to the actress who played Peter, expressing her sadness. Blackie published several rhyme collections illustrated by Cicely. The Wall Street Crash plunged the world into the Great Depression.

1933 *He Leadeth Me* published by Blackie. *Arthur Rackham's Fairy Book* published.

1934 *A Flower Fairy Alphabet* published.

1937 Walt Disney released *Snow White and the Seven Dwarfs*, an animated feature film version of the Grimm's fairy tale.

1938 *The Lord of the Rushie River* published by Blackie.

1939 Britain and France declared war on Germany, beginning World War II.

1940 *Flower Fairies of the Trees* published.

1944 *Flower Fairies of the Garden* published.

1945 Germany surrendered on 8th May, or VE Day. Japan surrendered to the Allies on 14th August, bringing World War II to an end.

1946 *Groundsel and Necklaces*, now called *The Fairy Necklaces*, published by Blackie.

1948   *Flower Fairies of the Wayside* published by Blackie.

1949   Disney released the animated film of the fairy tale *Cinderella*.
C. S. Lewis wrote *The Lion, the Witch and the Wardrobe*, the first of the *Chronicles of Narnia* fantasy stories.

1953   Disney released a technicolour, animated version of *Peter Pan*.

1961   Cicely moved to Storrington, Sussex.

1966   *The Fellowship of the Rings* published, the first book in *The Lord of the Rings* trilogy by J. R. R. Tolkien.

1973   Cicely Mary Barker died in Storrington, Sussex.

1985   *Flower Fairies of the Winter* published, featuring apposite fairies compiled from the seven existing Flower Fairies books.

1990   Frederick Warne acquired rights from Blackie and published new editions of the eight Flower Fairies books.

1991   *Hook*, a feature film retelling of *Peter Pan*, released by director Steven Spielberg.

1997   *Fairytale: A True Story*, a film based on the Cottingley case, released.

1998   *Flower Fairies of the Spring* celebrated the 75th anniversary of its first publication.

~ The Making of a Flower Fairy ~

Dorothy Barker is pictured here with children from the kindergarten that she ran. Cicely frequently used her sister's pupils as models for the Flower Fairies.

Like the Pre-Raphaelite artists whom she admired, Cicely Mary Barker painted directly from nature and paid scrupulous attention to detail. The next few pages trace the artistic progression from flower to Flower Fairy. Cicely filled at least one sketchbook a year for all of her working life, leaving behind a rich collection of botanical drawings that help reveal how she worked. Though Cicely's Flower Fairies look delightfully effortless and whimsical, they are actually the result of painstaking craftsmanship.

Many of Cicely's sketches of flowers, drawn on her countryside holidays, are very polished and closely resemble the depiction of the plants in the final Flower Fairies paintings. These detailed preparatory sketches allowed Cicely to concentrate on her models when she returned to her studio. Cicely drew her fairies from child models, but sadly few records exist of these preliminary sketches. Using Dion Clayton Calthrop's *English Costume* as reference, Cicely designed costumes for her models which echoed the colour, texture and shape of the flowers.

Flower Fairies of the Winter was compiled from the existing seven books in 1985. To create eight books of equal length, some of Cicely Mary Barker's original Flower Fairies were omitted from the new editions for editorial reasons. The out-of-print Flower Fairies featured on the following six pages exemplify Cicely's technique and highlight the botanical accuracy that was her hallmark.

These sketches, drawn sometime between 1919 and 1922, show Cicely's adeptness at capturing children in motion.

25

~ Scentless Mayweed ~

The Flower

This daisy-like flower is so-called to distinguish it from related plants with a strong smell. Blossoming between June and October, Scentless Mayweed grows on coastal cliffs. It is very likely that Cicely sketched Scentless Mayweed on one of her many seaside holidays.

The Sketch

Cicely first sketched the flower's shape in pencil and then enhanced the form with colour. This pencil and watercolour sketch of Scentless Mayweed is a typical example of Cicely's method. Because the flower has white petals, Cicely shaded the background grey to provide contrast and brushed the petals with light brown paint for depth. A few, quick lines capably convey the plant's spiky leaves.

The SCENTLESS MAYWEED Fairy

The Painting

The Scentless Mayweed Fairy was included in the 1948 edition of *Flower Fairies of the Wayside*. In her introduction to the book, Cicely urged her readers to notice, 'How pretty common things can be!' Against a background of spiny leaves and stems, the Scentless Mayweed Fairy dances in the foreground, a graceful reminder of wayside flowers' oft-overlooked beauty.

Active like most of the *Wayside* fairies, the Scentless Mayweed Fairy holds her flower petal skirt and skips daintily across the page. Fashioned from green, spear-like leaves, her bodice is topped with a collar made from Scentless Mayweed stems. A flower-head bonnet crowns the ensemble, and juxtaposes the delicate flower with its common surroundings.

27

~ Convolvulus ~

The Flower

Convolvulus, also called field bindweed, flowers between June and September. The plant's tenacity makes it a garden nuisance, despite its pretty, sweet-smelling flowers. Convolvulus can grow nearly anywhere—from gardens to waste grounds—stubbornly creeping over any obstacle in its path and climbing to heights of two metres.

The Sketch

This pencil sketch displays Cicely's care and skill in reproducing the complicated form of these funnel-shaped flowers. In this sketch from 1920, Cicely drew Convolvulus from various angles. She also sketched examples of buds, enabling her to depict an entire vine of Convolvulus in the final painting. By drawing the veiny leaves and the flowers' pistils in minute detail, Cicely achieved great delicacy in the final painting.

The Painting

Cicely Mary Barker painted the Convolvulus Fairy for the first edition of *Flower Fairies of the Summer*, published in 1925. This watercolour illustration is a fine example of Cicely's early Flower Fairies. The pink and white flowers tumble in a diagonal from the top right-hand corner, suggesting the plant's rapid spread. Cicely creates another diagonal, running from the fairy's hat to the blossom he is smelling, which directs the viewer's eye into the middle of the composition. Cicely's costume design cleverly suggests the flower's appearance with loose, ruffled sleeves and a belt made from a length of stem. The plant's trumpet-shaped flower makes a perfect cap for the Convolvulus Fairy. Down on his hands and knees, the boy's pose mimicks bindweed's crawl over the ground. Details such as the boy's dimpled elbow and the flower's stamens demonstrate Cicely's equal skill at painting children and botany.

~ Cat's Ear ~

The Flower

Cat's-Ear resembles a dandelion, but has a taller stalk. Flourishing anywhere from meadows to dunes and roadsides, this attractive yellow weed flowers in clusters between June and September.

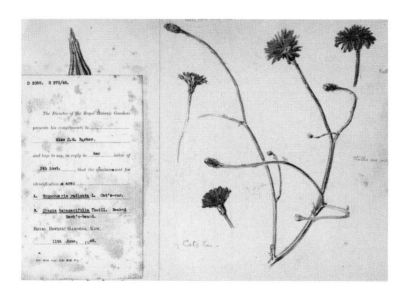

The Sketch

In the margins of her watercolour sketches, Cicely often wrote descriptive comments such as, 'buds have white hairs', to refresh her memory when she returned to her studio. When she could not identify a plant specimen, Cicely read *Wild Flowers as they Grow* by G. Clarke Nuttall or referred to the staff at Kew Gardens. As the letter attached to this sketch shows, Cicely sent samples of Cat's-Ear and Beaked Hawk's-Beard to the Royal Botanical Gardens in 1946 for identification. This sketch served as preparation for *Flower Fairies of the Wayside*, in which the Cat's-Ear fairy originally appeared.

The CAT'S-EAR Fairy

The Painting

The Cat's-Ear Fairy remains a pleasure to behold. Balancing on the stem with one arm reaching upwards, the fairy's extended pose reflects the plant's tall stalk. She wears a skirt made from an upside-down flower, with a shirt devised from the sepals. The Cat's-Ear Fairy grasps the entwined stems and camouflages herself behind the flowers. Eyes cast downwards, the Cat's-Ear Fairy smiles enigmatically and reminds the viewer of the elusive, hidden nature of the fairy world.

~ Spring Songs ~

Legend has it that fairies love music and dancing of all kinds, from lively reels to melancholy airs. Cicely Mary Barker's Flower Fairies are no exception and they made natural illustrations for sheet music. Cicely selected poems and pictures from *Flower Fairies of the Spring* and Olive Linnell set the verses to music. Their collaboration resulted in a music book entitled *Spring Songs with Music*, which was published by Blackie in 1924.

The Song of the Daisy Fairy

Very lightly and simply.

Come to me and play with me, I'm the ba-bies' flow - er; Make a neck-lace gay with me Spend the whole long day with me, Till the sun - set hour.

32

The book's popularity led to the publication of a further three music books in the twenties: *Summer Songs with Music*, *Autumn Songs with Music* and the compilation *Flower Songs of the Seasons*. In *Spring Songs*, Olive Linnell's music works harmoniously with the poems and pictures to bring the 12 Flower Fairies' personalities to life in a new medium. *The Song of the Daisy Fairy*, for example, is a suitably light and simple melody to accompany 'the babies' flower'. Although fairy melodies were once believed fatal to human ears, it is safe to assume that Linnell's sweet composition is harmless!

~ Spring Magic ~

The World is very old;
    But year by year
It groweth new again
    When buds appear.

The World is very old,
    And sometimes sad;
But when the daisies come
    The World is glad.

The World is very old;
    But every Spring
It groweth young again,
    And fairies sing.

FLOWER FAIRIES
of the SPRING

The Crocus Fairies

~ The Song of ~
The Crocus Fairies

Crocus of yellow, new and gay;
Mauve and purple, in brave array;
    Crocus white
    Like a cup of light,—
Hundreds of them are smiling up,
Each with a flame in its shining cup,
By the touch of the warm and welcome sun
Opened suddenly. Spring's begun!
Dance then, fairies, for joy, and sing
The song of the coming again of Spring.

~ The Song of ~
The Colt's~Foot Fairy

The winds of March are keen and cold;
I fear them not, for I am bold.

I wait not for my leaves to grow;
They follow after: they are slow.

My yellow blooms are brave and bright;
I greet the Spring with all my might.

The Colt's~Foot Fairy

~ The Song of ~
The Hazel~Catkin Fairy

Like little tails of little lambs,
   On leafless twigs my catkins swing;
They dingle-dangle merrily
   Before the wakening of Spring.

Beside the pollen-laden tails
   My tiny crimson tufts you see
The promise of the autumn nuts
   Upon the slender hazel tree.

While yet the woods lie grey and still
   I give my tidings: 'Spring is near!'
One day the land shall leap to life
   With fairies calling: 'Spring is HERE!'

40

The Hazel~Catkin Fairy.

The Hazel~Catkin Fairy

The Dog~Violet Fairy

~ THE SONG of ~
THE DOG~VIOLET FAIRY

The wren and robin hop around;
    The Primrose-maids my neighbours be;
The sun has warmed the mossy ground;
Where Spring has come, I too am found:
    The Cuckoo's call has wakened me!

~ The Song of ~
The Willow~Catkin Fairy

The people call me Palm, they do;
They call me Pussy-willow too.
And when I'm full in bloom, the bees
Come humming round my yellow trees.

The people trample round about
And spoil the little trees, and shout;
My shiny twigs are thin and brown:
The people pull and break them down.

To keep a Holy Feast, they say,
They take my pretty boughs away.
I should be glad—I should not mind—
If only people weren't unkind.

Oh, you may pick a piece, you may
(So dear and silky, soft and grey);
But if you're rough and greedy, why
You'll make the little fairies cry.

(This catkin is the flower of the Sallow Willow.)

The Willow~Catkin Fairy

The
Stitchwort
Fairy.

The Stitchwort Fairy

46

~ The Song of ~
The Stitchwort Fairy

I am brittle-stemmed and slender,
But the grass is my defender.

On the banks where grass is long,
I can stand erect and strong.

All my mass of starry faces
Looking up from wayside places,

From the thick and tangled grass,
Gives you greeting as you pass.

(A prettier name for Stitchwort is Starwort,
but it is not so often used.)

~ The Song of ~
The Windflower Fairy

While human-folk slumber,
　　The fairies espy
Stars without number
　　Sprinkling the sky.

The Winter's long sleeping,
　　Like night-time, is done;
But day-stars are leaping
　　To welcome the sun.

Star-like they sprinkle
　　The wildwood with light;
Countless they twinkle—
　　The Windflowers white!

('Windflower' is another name for Wood Anemone.)

The Windflower Fairy

The Wood~Sorrel Fairy

~ The Song of ~
The Wood~Sorrel Fairy

In the wood the trees are tall,
   Up and up they tower;
You and I are very small—
   Fairy-child and flower.

Bracken stalks are shooting high,
   Far and far above us;
We are little, you and I,
   But the fairies love us.

~ THE SONG of ~
THE DAISY FAIRY

Come to me and play with me,
    I'm the babies' flower;
Make a necklace gay with me,
Spend the whole long day with me,
    Till the sunset hour.

I must say Good-night, you know,
    Till tomorrow's playtime;
Close my petals tight, you know,
Shut the red and white, you know,
    Sleeping till the daytime.

The Daisy Fairy

The Dandelion Fairy

54

~ THE SONG of ~
THE DANDELION FAIRY

Here's the Dandelion's rhyme:
    See my leaves with tooth-like edges;
Blow my clocks to tell the time;
    See me flaunting by the hedges,
In the meadow, in the lane,
    Gay and naughty in the garden;
Pull me up—I grow again,
    Asking neither leave nor pardon.
Sillies, what are you about
    With your spades and hoes of iron?
You can never drive me out—
    Me, the dauntless Dandelion!

~ The Song of ~
The Daffodil Fairy

I'm everyone's darling: the blackbird and
    starling
Are shouting about me from blossoming
    boughs;
For I, the Lent Lily, the Daffy-down-dilly,
Have heard through the country the call to
    arouse.
The orchards are ringing with voices
    a-singing
The praise of my petticoat, praise of my
    gown;
The children are playing, and hark! they are
    saying
That Daffy-down-dilly is come up to town!

The Daffodil Fairy

The Celandine Fairy

~ THE SONG of ~
THE CELANDINE FAIRY

Before the hawthorn leaves unfold,
Or buttercups put forth their gold,
By every sunny footpath shine
The stars of Lesser Celandine.

The Primrose Fairy

~ The Song of ~
The Primrose Fairy

The Primrose opens wide in spring;
    Her scent is sweet and good:
It smells of every happy thing
    In sunny lane and wood.
I have not half the skill to sing
    And praise her as I should.

She's dear to folk throughout the land;
    In her is nothing mean:
She freely spreads on every hand
    Her petals pale and clean.
And though she's neither proud nor grand,
    She is the Country Queen.

~ The Song of ~
The Larch Fairy

Sing a song of Larch trees
    Loved by fairy-folk;
Dark stands the pinewood,
    Bare stands the oak,
But the Larch is dressed and trimmed
    Fit for fairy-folk!

Sing a song of Larch trees,
    Sprays that swing aloft,
Pink tufts, and tassels
    Grass-green and soft:
All to please the little elves
    Singing songs aloft!

The Larch Fairy

The Bluebell Fairy

~ The Song of ~
The Bluebell Fairy

My hundred thousand bells of blue,
    The splendour of the Spring,
They carpet all the woods anew
With royalty of sapphire hue;
The Primrose is the Queen, 'tis true.
    But surely I am King!
      Ah yes,
    The peerless Woodland King!

Loud, loud the thrushes sing their song;
    The bluebell woods are wide;
My stems are tall and straight and strong;
From ugly streets the children throng,
They gather armfuls, great and long,
    Then home they troop in pride—
      Ah yes,
    With laughter and with pride!

(This is the Wild Hyacinth.
The Bluebell of Scotland is the Harebell.)

~ The Song of ~
The May Fairy

My buds, they cluster small and green;
  The sunshine gaineth heat:
Soon shall the hawthorn tree be clothed
  As with a snowy sheet.

O magic sight, the hedge is white,
  My scent is very sweet;
And lo, where I am come indeed,
  The Spring and Summer meet.

The May Fairy

~ The Song of ~
The Speedwell Fairy

Clear blue are the skies;
    My petals are blue;
    As beautiful, too,
As bluest of eyes.

The heavens are high:
    By the field-path I grow
    Where wayfarers go,
And 'Good speed,' say I;

'See, here is a prize
    Of wonderful worth:
    A weed of the earth,
As blue as the skies!'

(There are many kinds of Speedwell:
this is the Germander.)

The Speedwell Fairy

The Lords~and~Ladies Fairy

~ The Song of ~
The Lords~and~Ladies Fairy

Here's the song of Lords-and-Ladies
    (in the damp and shade he grows):
I have neither bells nor petals,
    like the foxglove or the rose.
Through the length and breadth of England,
    many flowers you may see—
Petals, bells, and cups in plenty—
    but there's no one else like me.

In the hot-house dwells my kinsman,
    Arum-lily, white and fine;
I am not so tall and stately,
    but the quaintest hood is mine;
And my glossy leaves are handsome;
    I've a spike to make you stare;
And my berries are a glory in September.
    (BUT BEWARE!)

(The Wild Arum has other names besides Lords-and-Ladies,
  such as Cuckoo-Pint and Jack-in-the-Pulpit.)

~ The Song of ~ The Cowslip Fairy

The land is full of happy birds
And flocks of sheep and grazing herds.

I hear the songs of larks that fly
Above me in the breezy sky.

I hear the little lambkins bleat;
My honey-scent is rich and sweet.

Beneath the sun I dance and play
In April and in merry May.

The grass is green as green can be;
The children shout at sight of me.

The Cowslip Fairy

The Heart's~Ease Fairy

~ The Song of ~
The Heart's-Ease Fairy

Like the richest velvet
     (I've heard the fairies tell)
Grow the handsome pansies
     within the garden wall;
When you praise their beauty,
     remember me as well—
Think of little Heart's-Ease,
     the brother of them all!

Come away and seek me
     when the year is young,
Through the open ploughlands
     beyond the garden wall;
Many names are pretty
     and many songs are sung:
Mine—because I'm Heart's-Ease—
     are prettiest of all!

(An old lady says that when she was a little girl the children's
name for the Heart's-Ease or Wild Pansy was
Jump-up-and-kiss-me!)

75

~ The Song of ~
The Lady's~Smock Fairy

Where the grass is damp and green,
Where the shallow streams are flowing,
Where the cowslip buds are showing,
    I am seen.

Dainty as a fairy's frock,
White or mauve, of elfin sewing,
'Tis the meadow-maiden growing—
    Lady's-smock.

The Lady's-Smock Fairy

Spring Goes, Summer Comes

The little darling, Spring,
  Has run away;
The sunshine grew too hot for her to stay.

She kissed her sister, Summer,
  And she said:
"When I am gone, you must be queen
  instead."

Now reigns the Lady Summer,
  Round whose feet
A thousand fairies flock with blossoms sweet.

FLOWER FAIRIES
of the SUMMER

The Buttercup Fairy

~ The Song of ~
The Buttercup Fairy

'Tis I whom children love the best;
　My wealth is all for them;
For them is set each glossy cup
　Upon each sturdy stem.

O little playmates whom I love!
　The sky is summer-blue,
And meadows full of buttercups
　Are spread abroad for you.

~ The Song of ~
The Herb Robert Fairy

Little Herb Robert,
    Bright and small,
Peeps from the bank
    Or the old stone wall.

Little Herb Robert,
    His leaf turns red;
He's wild geranium,
    So it is said.

The Herb Robert Fairy

The Forget-me-not Fairy

~ THE SONG of ~
THE FORGET-ME-NOT FAIRY

So small, so blue, in grassy places
    My flowers raise
    Their tiny faces.

By streams my bigger sisters grow,
    And smile in gardens,
    In a row.

I've never seen a garden plot;
    But though I'm small
    Forget me not!

~ Buttercup ~

Ranunculus bulbosus

The Buttercup belongs to the Ranunculus family. There are three widespread native species of Buttercup: the bulbous Buttercup, the meadow Buttercup and the creeping Buttercup. All have flowers with five shiny yellow petals and five green sepals, differing mainly in their foliage and root systems. Although very pretty, and delightful as wayside flowers, Buttercups can be a nuisance in the garden where their growth can be invasive.

~ Herb Robert ~

Geranium robertianum

Herb Robert is part of the Geranium family, which includes the common wayside flowers known as Crane's-bill and Stork's-bill. All wild Geraniums have seed-pods with a long 'beak', which easily explains the bird references in the names.

As well as our native wild Geraniums, there are over a hundred species of perennial herbacious plants belonging to the same family. Hardy Geraniums tolerate most soil conditions but prefer good drainage. They will grow in both full sun and shade, depending on the variety.

~ Forget-me-not ~

Myosotis arvensis

The sky-blue flowers of the Forget-me-not are a welcome sight in early summer. They make good companion planting for tulips, as well as covering up the fading foliage of early crocuses and snowdrops. Forget-me-nots are easily grown from seed, either sown into nursery beds or scattered through the border. Once the foliage begins to fade the plants look untidy and can be removed, shaking the seed heads where desired in order to ensure new plants for the following year. Forget-me-nots can also have pink or white flowers, but blue is the traditional colour.

There are several stories in folklore about how the Forget-me-not got its name, but the most popular originated in Austria. Two young lovers were wandering along the banks of the Danube when the girl spotted a beautiful plant with tiny blue flowers floating down the river and said how sorry she was to see it being swept away. Her lover dived into the river and swam out to retrieve the flower, but as he made his way back he was sucked into a treacherous current and swept to his death. With the last of his strength he flung the flower into the hands of his lover and cried 'Vergiss mein nicht!': Forget me not.

The Poppy Fairy

~ THE SONG of ~
THE POPPY FAIRY

The green wheat's a-growing,
　　The lark sings on high;
In scarlet silk a-glowing,
　　Here stand I.

The wheat's turning yellow,
　　Ripening for sheaves;
I hear the little fellow
　　Who scares the bird-thieves.

Now the harvest's ended,
　　The wheat-field is bare;
But still, red and splendid,
　　I am there.

~ The Song of ~
The Foxglove Fairy

"Foxglove, Foxglove,
    What do you see?"
The cool green woodland,
    The fat velvet bee;
Hey, Mr Bumble,
    I've honey here for thee!

"Foxglove, Foxglove,
    What see you now?"
The soft summer moonlight
    On bracken, grass, and bough;
And all the fairies dancing
    As only they know how.

The Foxglove Fairy

~ Poppy ~

Papaver rhoeas

Poppies are some of the most beautiful of our native plants. Once commonly seen in cornfields, modern farming methods have reduced their numbers dramatically, although they can still be found in pockets along field margins and by the wayside. The elegantly branched, bristly stems bear magnificent scarlet flowers, up to eight centimetres across. The black stamens provide a wonderful contrast with the petals.

The Poppy has come to symbolise remembrance this century, being strongly identified with the fallen of two world wars. Every year many people wear a Poppy in their button-hole on Remembrance Sunday and give donations to charities supporting the veterans of war.

The Papaver family includes the well-loved garden flower, the oriental Poppy. A brilliantly coloured perennial, native to Asia Minor, it can grow as high as three or four feet. Originally orange-scarlet, with a deep purple base, the flowers are now also available in salmon-pink, bright crimson and white. These plants will grow in any good deep garden soil, but prefer to be left undisturbed. Most require staking.

All native Poppies contain a narcotic substance in their stems, and the opium Poppy is named for its derivative. The opium made from these Poppies was a great boon to medicine by helping to relieve pain as far back as the Middle Ages.

~ Foxglove ~

Digitalis purpurea

There are two theories to explain whence the Foxglove derived its name. The first claims that Foxglove is a corruption of 'little-folk's gloves' because the fairies wear its flowers as gloves or hats. However, some people believe that the flower earned its name because sly foxes used its blossoms as gloves to muffle their tread when out stealing chickens! Whichever derivation you prefer, Foxglove is a much nicer name than this fairy flower's other names – Goblin's Gloves, Witches' Thimbles and even Dead Man's Fingers.

It is possible that the Foxglove was given these other, sinister names because it is poisonous. It contains digitalis, a chemical that has proved remarkably helpful in stabilising heart conditions, but which can be fatal if taken in too great a quantity.

The wild Foxglove hardly differs from its garden cousins. Both are biennial, flowering in the second year of growth, and both prefer a sheltered location, either in sun or semi-shade. The wild Foxglove's distinctive purple blossoms are often seen in open woodland. Another foxglove, *Digitalis Lutea*, native to France and Belgium but now naturalised in chalky areas in Britain, is yellow. The choice of colours for the garden now extends to apricot, white and different shades of pink and purple. Whatever the colour, the Foxglove's stately spires add height and grace to the summer border.

The Wild Rose Fairy

~ The Song of ~
The Wild Rose Fairy

I am the queen whom everybody knows:
      I am the English Rose;
As light and free as any Jenny Wren,
      As dear to Englishmen;
As joyous as a Robin Redbreast's tune,
      I scent the air of June;
My buds are rosy as a baby's cheek;
      I have one word to speak,
One word which is my secret and my song,
'Tis "England, England, England" all day long.

~ The Song of ~
The White Clover Fairy

I'm little White Clover, kind and clean;
Look at my threefold leaves so green;
Hark to the buzzing of hungry bees:
"Give us your honey, Clover, please!"

Yes, little bees, and welcome, too!
My honey is good, and meant for you!

The White Clover Fairy

The Honeysuckle Fairy

~ The Song of ~
The Honeysuckle Fairy

The lane is deep, the bank is steep,
    The tangled hedge is high;
And clinging, twisting, up I creep,
    And climb towards the sky.
O Honeysuckle, mounting high!
O Woodbine, climbing to the sky!

The people in the lane below
    Look up and see me there,
Where I my honey-trumpets blow,
    Whose sweetness fills the air.
O Honeysuckle, waving there!
O Woodbine, scenting all the air!

~ The Song of ~
The Bird's-foot Trefoil Fairy

Here I dance in a dress like flames,
And laugh to think of my comical names.
Hoppetty hop, with nimble legs!
Some folks call me *Bacon and Eggs*!
While other people, it's really true,
Tell me I'm *Cuckoo's Stockings* too!
Over the hill I skip and prance;
I'm *Lady's Slipper,* and so I dance,
Not like a lady, grand and proud,
But to the grasshoppers' chirping loud.
My pods are shaped like a dicky's toes:
That is what *Bird's-Foot Trefoil* shows;
This is my name which grown-ups use,
But children may call me what they choose.

The Bird's-foot Trefoil Fairy

~ *Wild Rose* ~

Rosa rubiginosa

The Sweet Briar is native to Britain and one of the flowers most loved by poets. The Rose is a shrub with strong, arching stems, up to 1.5 metres tall, with apple-scented leaves. The flowers are pink with numerous yellow stamens, covering the shrub in profusion in early summer.

Once the petals have fallen the hips turn red and give a continued show into the autumn. In earlier times the hips would be collected and made into rose-hip syrup and rose-water.

~ *White Clover* ~

Trifolium repens

White Clover is one of the most important fodder plants and is frequently sown in pastures and in hay meadows. As Cicely's rhyme indicates, it is also loved by bees and gives a sweet, aromatic flavour to honey. It is a lovely treat for domestic pets such as rabbits and guinea-pigs.

Although an unwelcome intruder on a well-kept lawn, Clover is an easily recognisable and widespread wayside plant.

~ Honeysuckle ~
Lonicera periclymenum

Honeysuckle, or Woodbine, is a favourite wayside and garden plant. Its yellow or purple flowers are sweetly-scented and scramble happily through hedges and over trellises. The flowers are followed by small red or purple berries which stay on the plant into the winter.

Popular garden Honeysuckles include the Winter Honeysuckle, *Lonicera x purpusii*. Vigorous, and with a spreading habit, it is mainly grown for its small, sweetly fragrant white flowers.

~ Bird's-foot Trefoil ~
Lotus corniculatus

This little yellow flower has a host of different names. Its most common name, Bird's-foot Trefoil, refers to the elongated seed pods that spread stiffly out from the stalk like the toes of a sparrow from its leg. The buds are deep red and flattened, vaguely resembling rashers of bacon. As they are mixed with the egg-yolk coloured open flowers, this explains the particularly curious nickname, Bacon and Eggs!

Bird's-foot Trefoil is widespread in Britain but is often partially hidden amongst taller grasses.

The Nightshade Fairy

~ THE SONG of ~
THE NIGHTSHADE FAIRY

My name is Nightshade, also Bittersweet;
    Ah, little folk, be wise!
Hide you your hands behind you when we meet,
    Turn you away your eyes.
My flowers you shall not pick, nor berries eat,
    For in them poison lies.

(Though this is so poisonous, it is not the
Deadly Nightshade, but the Woody Nightshade.
The berries turn red a little later on.)

~ The Song of ~
The Harebell Fairy

O bells, on stems so thin and fine!
    No human ear
    Your sound can hear,
O lightly chiming bells of mine!

When dim and dewy twilight falls,
    Then comes the time
    When harebells chime
For fairy feasts and fairy balls.

They tinkle while the fairies play,
    With dance and song,
    The whole night long,
Till daybreak wakens, cold and grey,
And elfin music fades away.

(The Harebell is the Bluebell of Scotland.)

The Harebell Fairy

The Heather Fairy

~ The Song of ~ The Heather Fairy

"Ho, Heather, ho! From south to north
Spread now your royal purple forth!
Ho, jolly one! From east to west,
The moorland waiteth to be dressed!"

I come, I come! With footsteps sure
I run to clothe the waiting moor;
From heath to heath I leap and stride
To fling my bounty far and wide.

(The Heather in the picture is Bell Heather,
or Heath; it is different from the common
Heather which is also called Ling.)

~ Nightshade ~

Solanum dulcamara

The poisonous Woody Nightshade or Bittersweet is part of the Solanum, or Potato family.

The flowers are very attractive and scramble over small trees and shrubs. Woody Nightshade has purple petals that turn back on themselves to reveal the yellow anthers protruding in a yellow cone. After flowering the plant bears red berries.

Closely related to the Woody Nightshade is the Black Nightshade whose globular black berries give it its name.

Perhaps the best known of the Nightshade family is the Deadly Nightshade. This plant looks very different from its namesakes, being a stout, shrubby-looking plant with long drooping bell-shaped flowers of brown-ish purple or green. These are followed by glossy black berries. The whole plant is very poisonous and should not be touched.

Two striking garden plants belong to the Potato family: *Solanum crispum* and *Solanum jasminoides*. The former is a vigorous scrambling shrub that can be evergreen in warmer areas. Loose clusters of purple and yellow star-shaped flowers appear over a long period in summer. The stems need tying to a support. *Solanum jasminoides* is similar in appearance but is of a climbing habit. Semi-evergreen and slender-stemmed, it will grow vigorously through shrubs and over trellises. The purple and yellow flowers appear from early summer to autumn. There is also a delightful white form. All these plants need a sunny position to thrive and benefit from protection during the winter.

~ Harebell ~
Campanula rotundifolia

Although the Harebell is known as the Bluebell in Scotland, the two plants are unrelated. The Harebell is part of the Campanula or Bellflower family, and is a perennial plant that flowers in midsummer. The English Bluebell is a bulb that flowers in late spring. Superfically though, they look quite similar, with their delicate sky-blue drooping flowers and hairless stems. Cicely Mary Barker included the Bluebell fairy in *Flower Fairies of the Spring*.

~ Heather ~
Ranunculus bulbosus

All Heathers belong to the Erica family and require open situations and acid soil in which to thrive. They are widespread in Britain and dominant on heath and moorland, open woods and around bogs.

In the garden, Heathers are very popular for underplanting Rhododendrons and other lime-hating shrubs. The many different varieties offer different shades of red, purple, pink and white, and a careful selection of Heathers can guarantee blossoms in the garden all year round.

~ The Song of ~
The Yarrow Fairy

Among the harebells and the grass,
    The grass all feathery with seed,
I dream, and see the people pass:
    They pay me little heed.

And yet the children (so I think)
    In spite of other flowers more dear,
Would miss my clusters white and pink,
    If I should disappear.

(The Yarrow has another name, Milfoil,
which means Thousand Leaf; because her leaves
are all made up of very many tiny little leaves.)

The Yarrow Fairy

The Toadflax Fairy

~ THE SONG of ~
THE TOADFLAX FAIRY

The children, the children,
    they call me funny names,
They take me for their darling
    and partner in their games;
They pinch my flowers' yellow mouths,
    to open them and close,
Saying, *Snap-Dragon!*
      Toadflax!
        or, *darling Bunny-Nose!*

The Toadflax, the Toadflax,
    with lemon-coloured spikes,
With funny friendly faces
    that everybody likes,
Upon the grassy hillside
    and hedgerow bank it grows,
And it's *Snap-Dragon !*
      Toadflax!
        and *darling Bunny-Nose!*

~ The Song of ~
The Scabious Fairy

Like frilly cushions full of pins
For tiny dames and fairykins;

Or else like dancers decked with gems,
My flowers sway on slender stems.

They curtsey in the meadow grass,
And nod to butterflies who pass.

The Scabious Fairy

The Scarlet Pimpernel Fairy

~ The Song of ~
The Scarlet Pimpernel Fairy

By the furrowed fields I lie,
Calling to the passers-by:
"If the weather you would tell,
Look at Scarlet Pimpernel."

When the day is warm and fine,
I unfold these flowers of mine;
Ah, but you must look for rain
When I shut them up again!

Weather-glasses on the walls
Hang in wealthy people's halls:
Though I lie where cart-wheels pass
I'm the Poor Man's Weather-Glass!

~ Yarrow ~

Achillea millefolium

This strongly-scented, feathery-leaved plant is very common along the wayside and in open grassland. It is of an upright habit and has clusters of tiny creamy-white flowers bunched together into flat flower-heads.

Yarrow's garden relatives resemble their common cousin quite closely. Achillea 'Coronation Gold' and 'Gold Plate' are striking, long-flowering perennials that flourish happily in dry, stony soil. The sturdy stems do not require staking, and the plants will grow into thick clumps if left undisturbed.

~ Toadflax ~

Linaria vulgaris

The common Toadflax is a perennial plant with flowers like tiny yellow snapdragons, but with long spurs hanging from the lower lip. These contain nectar, and Toadflax is popular with bees. The unusual shape and bright yellow colour make it an attractive flower, and it is commonly found throughout most of Britain.

Its garden cousin, the Snapdragon (*Antirrhinum*), a popular summer annual bedding plant, shares the Toadflax's endearing ability to open and close its mouth if squeezed gently just at the point where the 'lips' join.

~ Scabious ~

Knautia arvensis

The field Scabious is common in pastures, on downlands and scrub, tolerating dry conditions and a chalky soil. It is a perennial with strong hairy stems, bearing flat-topped blue flowerheads on long stalks.

Scabious is a popular garden plant, preferring a good well-drained soil and flowering from June to October. *Scabiosa caucasica*, from the Caucasus, is perhaps the finest of the perennial species, reaching 90 centimetres in height. It has lavender-blue flowers up to 10 centimetres across.

~ Scarlet Pimpernel ~

Anagallis arvensis

This annual plant can easily be overlooked because of its prostrate, creeping habit. The plant is still common in cornfields and along the wayside despite the widespread use of modern herbicides. It is probably native to sand dunes and prefers sandy or chalky soil. The flowers are salmon-red rather than scarlet, and are borne singly on long stalks.

Cicely Mary Barker's rhyme discloses the Scarlet Pimpernel's useful habit of closing its flowers when rain is approaching.

~ The Song of ~
The Greater Knapweed Fairy

Oh, please, little children, take note of my
    name:
To call me a thistle is really a shame:
I'm harmless old Knapweed, who grows
    on the chalk,
I never will prick you when out for your
    walk.

Yet I should be sorry, yes, sorry indeed,
To cut your small fingers and cause them
    to bleed;
So bid me Good Morning when out for
    your walk,
And mind how you pull at my very tough
    stalk.

(Sometimes this Knapweed is called Hardhead;
and he has a brother, the little Knapweed, whose
flower is not quite like this.)

122

The Greater Knapweed Fairy

The Ragwort Fairy

~ The Song of ~
The Ragwort Fairy

Now is the prime of Summer past,
    Farewell she soon must say;
But yet my gold you may behold
    By every grassy way.

And what though Autumn comes apace,
    And brings a shorter day?
Still stand I here, your eyes to cheer,
    In gallant gold array.

~ The Song of ~
The Traveller's Joy Fairy

Traveller, traveller, tramping by
To the seaport town where the big ships lie,
See, I have built a shady bower
To shelter you from the sun or shower.
Rest for a bit, then on, my boy!
Luck go with you, and Traveller's Joy!

Traveller, traveller, tramping home
From foreign places beyond the foam,
See, I have hung out a white festoon
To greet the lad with the dusty shoon.
Somewhere a lass looks out for a boy:
Luck be with you, and Traveller's Joy!

(Traveller's Joy is Wild Clematis; and when the
flowers are over, it becomes a mass of silky fluff,
and then we call it Old-Man's-Beard.)

The Traveller's Joy Fairy

~ Greater Knapweed ~
Centaurea Scabiosa

The Greater Knapweed is common on chalk soils and lime grasslands in southern parts of Britain. The flowerheads are striking and showy, up to 5 centimetres wide, and flower in mid-summer.

The garden relative that most resembles the Knapweed is the perennial Cornflower (*Centaurea montana*). This long-standing garden favourite forms leafy clumps and produces large heads of blue flowers in early summer. It requires little care, is fully hardy, and will thrive in a sunny position.

~ Ragwort ~
Senecio jacobaea

This bright, sunny plant is common throughout Britain on roadsides, wasteland and in neglected pastures. It is a sturdy, erect perennial (sometimes biennial), that can reach a height of 1 metre. The flowers are bright yellow, with a daisy-like shape, and appear from mid-summer into autumn. Despite its cheerful appearance, Ragwort is poisonous to livestock, particularly horses, and should be removed from pasture before allowing animals to graze.

~ Traveller's Joy ~
Ranunculus bulbosus

The wild Clematis is a woody climbing shrub that scrambles happily through small trees, shrubs and hedges, giving all-year interest. As the rhyme indicates, the pretty, fragrant, creamy flowers give it the name of 'Traveller's Joy' in summer, while the feathery clusters of seed-heads, which give the appearance of clumps of fine hair on wood borders or hedges in autumn, are an obvious reason for its other name, 'Old Man's Beard'.

The flowers are freely borne in July and August, and are a familiar sight in chalk and limestone districts.

There are many different types of Clematis for gardens, enough to give all-year colour if planted with care. *Clematis montana* is a vigorous climber producing blankets of leafy growth and reaching up to 10 metres. The large spring flowers are borne in abundance and come in shades of white and pink, depending upon the named variety. It will grow happily in sun and partial shade.

The most popular Clematis varieties are the large-flowered hybrids. They come in almost all colours and are suitable both for training against a wall and for scrambling over large shrubs, seldom reaching a height of more than 3 metres.

The Rose Fairy

~ THE SONG of ~
THE ROSE FAIRY

Best and dearest flower that grows,
Perfect both to see and smell;
Words can never, never tell
Half the beauty of a Rose—
Buds that open to disclose
Fold on fold of purest white,
Lovely pink, or red that glows
Deep, sweet-scented. What delight
    To be Fairy of the Rose!

~ Rose ~

Rosa

The Rose is probably the single best-loved garden plant, famed not only for its beauty but also for its delicate fragrance. The red Rose has traditionally been associated with love and passion, and is now the most popular gift on Valentine's day. The white Rose is chiefly associated with purity: the two flowers most commonly symbolising the Virgin Mary are the Lily and the Rose.

The Rose also has an important place in British history. The famous Wars of the Roses were so named because the House of Lancaster's emblem was the red Rose; the House of York's emblem was the white. Henry VII (a Lancastrian) finally united the two houses by marrying Elizabeth of York and created a new emblem for the House of Tudor; the red and white Tudor Rose.

As befits the Rose's popularity, a Rose can be found for nearly every garden, from the useful ground cover Rose to the vigorous ramblers that can reach 10 metres in both height and spread. Roses have also been bred to have several different flower shapes, from the old 'cabbage' Rose to the pointed elegance of the hybrid Teas.

132

These Roses are some of the most popular of the different categories:

'Mme Isaac Pereire' (large shrub Rose)
A lovely bourbon Rose with vigorous, arching branches and richly fragrant flowers of a deep pink with magenta shading. It appears from summer into autumn and can attain a height of over 2 metres.

'Rosa Mundi' (small shrub Rose)
This well-known Rose was beloved in medieval times. It has double flowers of a pale pink with crimson stripes and will grow to 1 metre height and spread.

'Maigold' (climbing Rose)
A vigorous climber with thorny stems and lush foliage. Fragrant yellow blooms appear in early summer and, less profusely, in the autumn. It will achieve a height and spread of 4 metres.

'Albertine' (rambler)
An old and popular rambling Rose with richly fragrant, double salmon-pink flowers, freely borne in summer on vigorous growth of up to 5 metres height and spread. Although only once-flowering, the sheer profusion of colour and scent makes it a classic cottage garden Rose.

'Peace' (hybrid tea)
First launched in 1945, hence its name, this pinky-yellow Rose is a classic hybrid Tea. It has a good fragrance, strong growth and flowers from mid-summer to autumn.

~ The Lost Fairies ~

Flower Fairies of the Winter was compiled from the existing seven books in 1985. To create eight books of equal length, some of Cicely Mary Barker's original Flower Fairies were omitted from the new editions for editorial reasons, in some cases because the quality of the paintings had deteriorated. The following pages feature the five 'lost' fairies of *Flower Fairies of the Summer*.

The Convolvulus Fairy

The White Campion Fairy

The Sorrel Fairy

The Thistle Fairy

The Wild Thyme Fairy

THE BERRY-QUEEN

An elfin rout,
    With berries laden,
Throngs round about
    A merry maiden.

Red-gold her gown;
    Sun-tanned is she;
She wears a crown
    Of bryony.

The sweet Spring came,
    And lovely Summer:
Guess, then, her name—
    This latest-comer!

FLOWER FAIRIES
of the AUTUMN

The Mountain Ash Fairy

~ The Song of ~
The Mountain Ash Fairy

They thought me, once, a magic tree
    Of wondrous lucky charm,
And at the door they planted me
    To keep the house from harm.

They have no fear of witchcraft now,
    Yet here am I today;
I've hung my berries from the bough,
    And merrily I say:

"Come, all you blackbirds, bring your wives,
    Your sons and daughters too;
The finest banquet of your lives
    Is here prepared for you."

*(The Mountain Ash's other name is Rowan; and
it used to be called Witchentree and Witch-wood too.)*

~ The Song of ~
The Michaelmas Daisy Fairy

"Red Admiral, Red Admiral,
    I'm glad to see you here,
        Alighting on my daisies one by one!
I hope you like their flavour
    and although the Autumn's near,
        Are happy as you sit there in the sun?"

"I thank you very kindly, sir!
    Your daisies *are* so nice,
        So pretty and so plentiful are they;
The flavour of their honey, sir,
    it really does entice;
        I'd like to bring my brothers, if I may!"

"Friend butterfly, friend butterfly,
    go fetch them one and all!
        I'm waiting here to welcome every guest;
And tell them it is Michaelmas,
    and soon the leaves will fall,
        But *I* think Autumn sunshine is the best!"

The Michaelmas Daisy Fairy

145

~ Mountain Ash ~

Sorbus aucuparia

This neat, multi-stemmed tree is open and graceful, and attractive in every season. Clusters of creamy flowers in spring have a sweet, lingering fragrance, while the clusters of bright red berries and coppery leaf tones make it an eye-catching sight in the late summer and autumn. The elegant, curved stems are also stunning when silhouetted against a winter sky or rimed with frost. Found throughout Europe, the Mountain Ash, also known as the Rowan tree or Witch-wood, was popularly believed to protect against witchcraft, cure illness and even tell the future. Cicely Mary Barker alludes to this belief in her rhyme. However, folklore tells that the wood taken from the tree must not be cut with a metal instrument but broken off by hand, and the tree must be 'asked' to provide its power.

There are two principal cultivated varieties of Mountain Ash: 'Asplenifolia', which has more deeply cut leaflets, and 'Sheerwater Seedling'. The latter is good for a position where space is limited as its ascending branches give the tree a narrow crown. The average height of a Mountain Ash at 20 years is 5 metres, although it can eventually achieve 12 metres. Both the varieties named have fruits which colour orange-red in the autumn. Although inedible, the berries are not poisonous and make the tree a child-friendly choice for the garden.

~ Michaelmas Daisy ~

Aster novae-angliae

The Michaelmas Daisy is so popular in English cottage gardens that we are inclined to think it must be a native plant. Surprisingly, it was brought over from North America quite recently, and the banks of daisies seen flourishing along railway embankments are refugees from cultivation. Only one variety is really entitled to be called Michaelmas Daisy, because it is sacred to the Archangel Michael and always blooms on and around his day, 29 September. This particular plant is seldom seen, but its understudies make a fine show in the border.

Although the Michaelmas Daisies have only recently crossed the Atlantic, their close relatives, the asters or 'starworts', as they were known in England, have been here for many centuries. European girls have plucked petals from several kinds of asters in the game 'He loves me; he loves me not', and the Italian Starwort, *Aster amellus* was woven into wreaths and strewn on the altars of the gods in ancient Greece.

Some popular and mildew-resistant varieties of Michaelmas Daisy include the rose-pink 'Harrington's Pink', vivid cerise 'Andenken an Alma Potschke' and white 'Herbstschnee' ('Autumn Snow'). All these varieties grow to a height of approximately 1.2 metres and require very little staking.

~ The Song of ~
The Wayfaring Tree Fairy

My shoots are tipped with buds as dusty-grey
As ancient pilgrims toiling on their way.

Like Thursday's child with far to go, I stand,
All ready for the road to Fairyland;

With hood, and bag, and shoes, my name to suit,
And in my hand my gorgeous-tinted fruit.

The Wayfaring Tree Fairy

149

The Robin's Pincushion Fairy

~ THE SONG of ~
THE ROBIN'S PINCUSHION FAIRY

People come and look at me,
Asking who this rogue may be?
—Up to mischief, they suppose,
Perched upon the briar-rose.

I am nothing else at all
But a fuzzy-wuzzy ball,
Like a little bunch of flame;
I will tell you how I came:

First there came a naughty fly,
Pricked the rose, and made her cry;
Out I popped to see about it;
This is true, so do not doubt it!

~ Wayfaring Tree ~

Viburnum lantana

This many-branched deciduous shrub is a common sight in Southern England, preferring chalky soil and mixed woodland. The young twigs are covered with grey hairs and the leaves have a wrinkled, felted appearance. The flowers appear in mid-summer, covering the shrub in flat, creamy-white flowerheads, but the Wayfaring Tree comes into its own in the autumn, when the 'gorgeous-tinted fruit' gleams red, yellow and black in great profusion.

The cultivated varieties of Viburnum offer a tremendous diversity of foliage, flowers and fruit and make handsome features in a garden. Hardy and easy to grow, they provide year-round colour and interest.

Viburnum x bodnantense 'Dawn' has sweetly scented rose-red flowers in bud, opening to soft pink from early winter to early spring. The young foliage is tinged with bronze. Ultimate height, 3 metres.

Viburnum x davidii is a low-growing, densely branched evergreen shrub, with leathery, dark green leaves. Small white flowers are borne in flat heads in early summer, followed by glowing blue fruits that last throughout the winter. Ultimate height, 1.5 metres.

~ Robin's Pincushion ~

Diplolepis rosae

This is perhaps the most unexpected of all the Flower Fairies. It is in fact an imposter and not a flower at all! The Robin's Pincushion is a gall caused by a tiny wasp. It is common on all different kinds of roses, but is most frequently seen on Dog Roses. The gall can be of varying size and colour and is covered with long, branching hairs. In the autumn it hardens to a dry, brown structure that remains on the plant all winter.

Cicely gives us clues to the origin of the gall in her rhyme. 'First there came a naughty fly,/Pricked the rose and made her cry.' The female wasp punctures the soft plant tissue, often a bud, creating the gall structure in which she then lays her eggs. The developing larvae each have a separate chamber. At the end of the summer the larvae become pupae which overwinter in the gall. The wasps then leave in the spring. They live exclusively on the roses until they are fully adult, but they do not do their hosts any significant damage, though the galls can look unsightly.

The Elderberry Fairy

~ THE SONG of ~
THE ELDERBERRY FAIRY

Tread quietly:
O people, hush!
—For don't you see
A spotted thrush,
One thrush or two,
Or even three,
In every laden elder-tree?

They pull and lug,
They flap and push,
They peck and tug
To strip the bush;
They have forsaken
Snail and slug;
Unseen I watch them, safe and snug!

(These berries do us no harm, though they don't taste very nice.
Country people make wine from them; and boys make
whistles from elder stems.)

~ The Song of ~
The Dogwood Fairy

I was a warrior,
　　When, long ago,
Arrows of Dogwood
　　Flew from the bow.
Passers-by, nowadays,
　　Go up and down,
Not one remembering
　　My old renown.

Yet when the Autumn sun
　　Colours the trees,
Should you come seeking me,
　　Know me by these:
Bronze leaves and crimson leaves,
　　Soon to be shed;
Dark little berries,
　　On stalks turning red.

(Cornel is another name for Dogwood; and Dogwood has nothing to do
with dogs. It used to be Dag-wood, or Dagger-wood, which, with another
name, Prickwood, show that it was used to make sharp-pointed things.)

The Dogwood Fairy

The Acorn Fairy

~ The Song of ~
The Acorn Fairy

To English folk the mighty oak
  Is England's noblest tree;
Its hard-grained wood is strong and good
  As English hearts can be.
And would you know how oak-trees grow,
  The secret may be told:
You do but need to plant for seed
  One acorn in the mould;
For even so, long years ago,
  Were born the oaks of old.

~ Elder ~

Sambucus nigra

Much-loved residents of the English hedgerows, elders have long been cultivated for their pretty flowers and berries. The European Elder is commonly found throughout England, covering wasteland and other neglected areas with its scented, creamy-white blossom. Both the elderflowers and elderberries have been used for centuries to make country wines, once used as medicines for sleeplessness and gout. However, country people believed that the sweet fragrance of the flowers could poison anyone unwary enough to fall asleep beneath an Elder tree.

There are many hardy species of elder, but generally only the cultivars of the European Elder and the Red Elder (*Sambucus racemosa*) are grown in Britain, making a colourful summer feature in an informal garden.

Sambucus nigra 'Aurea' is a very hardy variety, which needs full sun to develop the best golden colour. *Sambucus n.* 'Guincho Purple' bears foliage that starts green and develops into purple-black growth in summer, finally turning red in the autumn. The flowers are pinkish in bud, held on purple stalks. Both the above have an ultimate height of 7 metres.

An Elder Fairy, with her flower, appears in *Flower Fairies of the Trees*.

~ Dogwood ~

Cornus sanguinea

This attractive shrub is usually found in hedgerows or mixed woodland. The Latin name 'sanguinea' refers to the blood-red tinge seen on the twigs in autumn and winter which, along with the sprigs of creamy blossom in early summer and round black fruits in the autumn, gives Dogwood year-round interest.

As Cicely tells in her rhyme, Dogwood was used to make arrows because of its hard, smooth wood. The name refers to its use in making sharp-pointed things; thus Dagger-wood became Dag-wood, later corrupted to Dogwood.

There are many varieties of *Cornus*, all of which are grown for their abundant flowers, their brilliant winter-stem colour and their foliage. They are all quite hardy, native to northern climes, and they are mainly deciduous shrubs and small trees.

The Red-barked Dogwood (*Cornus alba*) is best grown as a multi-stemmed plant. It is very vigorous and spreads by suckers. The crimson-red stems show their richest colour when pruned regularly. The leaves turn bright crimson and purple in autumn, and flattened clusters of small yellow-white flowers in early summer are followed by pale blue-white berries.

The Cornelian Cherry (*Cornus mas*) is a small tree with spreading branches. 'Variegata' is a particularly attractive cultivar, which has a broad white margin to its grey-green leaves. It bears clusters of tiny golden yellow flowers, followed by bright red fruits in autumn.

~ The English Oak ~

Quercus robur

'To English folk the mighty oak/Is England's noblest tree.' The oak and the elm have long been considered the most English of trees, and after the dreadful ravages of Dutch Elm Disease, the oak now takes predominance. Two thousand years ago, much of the native forest was made up of oak trees, and they were regarded as sacred by Celtic and Scandinavian peoples. The Druids gathered in groves of oak and the tree still retains a tradition of magical power, perhaps because of its great longevity.

Probably the most famous oak tree is the Boscobel Oak. Charles II hid in this tree after the battle of Worcester in 1651 in order to escape the pursuing Parliamentarians. Royalists across the country wore oak leaves to celebrate his escape, and on 29 May 1660 when he returned to London to take back his throne, oak leaves were worn until midday, followed by ash leaves until sunset. Some people still wear an oak leaf on 29 May to keep the tradition alive.

The oak tree is valued above all for the high quality hardwood it produces. This became crucial to the English Navy when most of the timber used for the ships was oak. However, recent investigations by archeologists have revealed that not all the trees used were native. The *Mary Rose*, the flagship of Henry VIII, was discovered to be made from French Oak – rather ironic, given the hostilities between England and France at the time.

The oak leaf and acorn can frequently be found in stone and wood carvings in churches and in private houses. Pulpits and pews sometimes show oak boughs, and these can also be found decorating gravestones. Window cords and light pulls are often in the shape of an acorn, and oak leaf motifs have been popular in kitchens and pantries for many centuries. Oak trees are frequently found as the centrepiece in a public place, for example the village green or alongside a cricket pitch.

The oak tree is also known as a weather forecaster:

'If the Oak before the Ash

Then there'll only be a splash.

If the Ash before the Oak

Then prepare for a mighty soak.'

This rhyme predicts whether it will be a wet or dry summer by looking at which tree first shows its leaves in spring.

The English Oak is native to Britain. It has a broad crown and readily identifiable foliage. It is slow growing but very long-lived, and although it will grow to only 6 metres after 20 years, it can achieve an ultimate height of 32 metres.

A garden variety of *Quercus robur* is 'Concordia'. This is smaller than its parent, a rounded, slow-growing tree with upright golden foliage.

The Black Bryony Fairy

~ THE SONG of ~
THE BLACK BRYONY FAIRY

Bright and wild and beautiful
For the Autumn festival,
I will hang from tree to tree
Wreaths and ropes of Bryony,
To the glory and the praise
Of the sweet September days.

*(There is nothing black to be seen about this Bryony, but people do
say it has a black root; and this may be true, but you would need to
dig it up to find out. It used to be thought a cure for freckles.)*

The Horse Chestnut Fairy

~ The Song of ~
The Horse Chestnut Fairy

My conkers, they are shiny things,
    And things of mighty joy,
And they are like the wealth of kings
    To every little boy;
I see the upturned face of each
    Who stands around the tree:
He sees his treasure out of reach,
    But does not notice *me*.

For love of conkers bright and brown,
    He pelts the tree all day;
With stones and sticks he knocks them down,
    And thinks it jolly play.
But sometimes I, the elf, am hit
    Until I'm black and blue;
O laddies, only wait a bit,
    I'll shake them down to you!

~ Black Bryony ~
Tamus communis

Black Bryony belongs to a family of twining plants that spring from large tubers, or roots. It is a very common plant in woodland and hedgerows, twining its weak stems around anything within reach. The leaves are heart-shaped and very shiny, and late in the autumn they turn dark purple or bright yellow, which, along with the red berries, makes a dazzling display. Cicely quotes the country belief that Black Bryony's roots are black, and this is in fact quite true. The large root is black on the outside, though light yellow inside, and it was traditionally taken as a herbal remedy in diluted form. However, it would be unwise to try this as it is classed nowadays as an irritant poison and an overdose can even result in death. Children should be cautioned against eating the berries.

As an external remedy Black Bryony is said to be useful, helping to relieve the pain of gout and rheumatism. The root can also be scraped to a pulp and applied as a poultice to bruises. It is not the only 'cure for freckles'; it shares that characteristic with crushed strawberries!

Black Bryony's most useful cultivated relative is the Yam, which forms an important source of food in many tropical countries.

~ Horse Chestnut Tree ~

Aesculus hippocastanum

The Horse Chestnut tree is often seen in British parks and open spaces. Chestnuts can be used to create magnificent avenues, which look spectacular in May when the blossom is in full bloom. Despite its prevalence throughout Britain, the Horse Chestnut was originally brought back from India, East Asia and the Himalayas. Its exotic origins are displayed in the marvellous flower candles, which can be creamy-white or red. The tree's great gift to children is the leathery fruit containing the seed known as a 'conker'.

Cicely's rhyme refers to little boys pelting the trees with sticks in order to bring down as many conkers as possible. This is in order to play a traditional playground game, which involves threading the shiny brown conker on to a string and taking it in turns to hit other people's conkers; the winner being the child whose conker stays intact. It should be noted that conkers are poisonous to animals and humans.

The Horse Chestnut tree is far too big for most private gardens, but there are smaller trees and shrubs to choose from within the genus. *Aesculus parviflora* is a very free-flowering, vigorous, open shrub that bears white flower candles in mid to late summer. The mid-green leaves turn a glowing yellow in the autumn. The fruit is smooth and pear-shaped. This shrub will reach a height of approximately 2 metres after 10 years; ultimately 4 metres tall.

The Blackberry Fairy

~ The Song of ~
The Blackberry Fairy

My berries cluster black and thick
For rich and poor alike to pick.

I'll tear your dress, and cling, and tease,
And scratch your hands and arms and knees.

I'll stain your fingers and your face,
And then I'll laugh at your disgrace.

But when the bramble-jelly's made,
You'll find your trouble well repaid.

~ The Song of ~
The Nightshade Berry Fairy

"You see my berries, how they gleam and
    glow,
Clear ruby-red, and green, and orange-
    yellow;
Do they not tempt you, fairies, dangling so?"
    The fairies shake their heads and answer "No!
      You are a crafty fellow!"

"What, won't you try them? There is
    naught to pay!
Why should you think my berries poisoned
    things?
You fairies may look scared and fly away—
The children will believe me when I say
    My fruit is fruit for kings!"
    But all good fairies cry in anxious haste,
"O children, do not taste!"

(You must believe the good fairies, though the berries look nice.
This is the Woody Nightshade, which has purple and
yellow flowers in the summer.)

The Nightshade Berry Fairy

~ *Blackberry* ~
Rubus fruticosus

The Blackberry or bramble is found in woodland, hedgerows, heathland and gardens throughout Britain. The stems are covered with coarse prickles and scramble over the earth or through other shrubs and climbers. The white blossoms are very attractive and cover the plant in May and June. The fruit ripens from red to black and is ready to pick from August until October.

Blackberries are an old favourite in country areas, and entire families can often be seen picking the fruit from hedgerows. Some of the fruit is eaten raw, but many people prefer it in the traditional British pudding, Blackberry and Apple Pie. The cultivated Blackberries are the best varieties to plant in the garden.

~ *Woody Nightshade* ~
Solanum dulcamara

Woody Nightshade and Deadly Nightshade, although very different to look at, share a justly terrible reputation. Both are very dangerous: Deadly Nightshade is one of the most poisonous of European

174

wild plants and induces madness and hallucinations, sometimes fatal, while Woody Nightshade contains a powerful alkaloid that triggers muscle spasm and severe sickness. It may well be that Deadly Nightshade started the belief in witches flying on broomsticks. One of its hallucinogenic effects is said to be rather like a swooping, terrifying flight, and witches are believed to have used Deadly Nightshade in some of their potions. Woody Nightshade is not quite as harmful. The distilled juice of the herb was said to be good for ringworm, shingles and ear-ache. However, that was in a very dilute form; the berries are *extremely harmful* and should not be touched.

As Cicely says, the plant is very attractive to look at. She drew the Nightshade Fairy, with his purple and yellow flowers, in *Flower Fairies of the Summer*. The green berries turn yellow and then red when ripe. The garden varieties of *Solanum* are equally attractive, and some are very similar. *Solanum crispum* 'Glasnevin' has fragrant deep blue flower clusters with yellow centres that appear from mid summer to early autumn. The round white fruits are flushed with yellow. The stem is twining and has dark green leaves that are semi-evergreen. It does best in a sheltered situation and will achieve a height of 4 metres.

Solanum jasminoides 'Album' has star-like white blooms held in clusters throughout the summer. It is also semi-evergreen but is not frost-hardy.

The Rose Hip Fairy

~ The Song of ~
The Rose Hip Fairy

Cool dewy morning,
  Blue sky at noon,
White mist at evening,
  And large yellow moon;

Blackberries juicy
  For staining of lips;
And scarlet, O scarlet
  The Wild Rose Hips!

Gay as a gipsy
  All Autumn long,
Here on the hedge-top
  This is my song.

~ The Song of ~
The Crab-Apple Fairy

Crab-apples, Crab-apples, out in the wood,
Little and bitter, yet little and good!
The apples in orchards, so rosy and fine,
Are children of wild little apples like mine.

The branches are laden, and droop to the
     ground;
The fairy-fruit falls in a circle around;
Now all you good children, come gather
     them up:
They'll make you sweet jelly to spread
     when you sup.

One little apple I'll catch for myself;
I'll stew it, and strain it, to store on a shelf
In four or five acorn-cups, locked with a key
In a cupboard of mine at the root of the tree.

The Crab-Apple Fairy

The Hazel-Nut Fairy

~ The Song of ~
The Hazel-Nut Fairy

Slowly, slowly, growing
　　While I watched them well,
See, my nuts have ripened;
　　Now I've news to tell.
I will tell the Squirrel,
　　"Here's a store for you;
But, kind Sir, remember
　　The Nuthatch likes them too."

I will tell the Nuthatch,
　　"Now, Sir, you may come;
Choose your nuts and crack them,
　　But leave the children some."
I will tell the children,
　　"You may take your share;
Come and fill your pockets,
　　But leave a few to spare."

~ *Dog Rose* ~

Rosa canina

Roses have been cultivated in gardens for over 4000 years, bred from the wild roses found in different parts of the world. More than 150 varieties of wild rose have been discovered; some in Europe and the Middle East; others in the Far East and North America. There are many differences between them, but they all share one characteristic; the beautiful five-petalled flowers, often sweetly scented.

The Dog Rose is native to Britain and is common in deciduous woodland, hedgerows and thickets. It flowers only once, in early summer, but makes up for its brief flowering time with an abundant display of light pink or pale red flowers borne on its arching, thorny stems. The rose hips ripen to a rich red in late summer and autumn, providing a bountiful harvest for birds and small mammals. Rose hips are edible to humans too, though tart to taste, and can be used to make jelly and cordials.

There are several cultivated varieties of roses that look similar to the Dog Rose. *Rosa gallica* 'Complicata' has spectacular single, bright pink blooms with a boss of golden stamens held in its white centre. It has vigorous, arching branches, and is particularly effective when trained through an apple or pear tree. It flowers just once, in early summer, but its marvellous display makes it well worth considering as a climber for an informal garden setting.

Rosa rugosa 'Alba' flowers continuously from early summer to early autumn, followed by orange-red hips that may be carried alongside the late blooms. The flowers are white, single and sweetly scented. The *rugosa*

182

roses are very robust and do well in any soil. They are very spiny, but have a deep green, glossy foliage that is notably disease free and turns a rich gold in autumn. As well as being vigorous, colourful plants for the border, *rugosas* make excellent hedges.

~ Crab-Apple Tree ~

Malus sylvestris

These hardy, deciduous trees are a joy to behold in spring, covered in clouds of light pink blossom. The apple-like fruits ripen in early autumn and are green, flushed with red. Though edible, the fruit is hard and sour, and it is usually made into Crab-Apple jelly. Crab-Apples are common in England and Wales, becoming rarer in Scotland. They are most often found in deciduous woodland and hedgerows.

Tradition has it that girls should gather the fruit and arrange it to form their suitors' initials. Then they should hide it away until Michaelmas Day. At dawn on that day they should look at the fruit and see which initial has stayed in the best condition. Thus they will learn which of their suitors will become their husband.

There are many varieties of cultivated Crab-Apple. They are all easily grown and, being generally small, are suitable for most gardens. *Malus x robusta* 'Red Sentinel' is popular for its spectacular display of fruits in autumn. The frothy spring blossom is white. 'Red Sentinel' will reach an ultimate height of 6 metres.

Malus x zumi 'Golden Hornet' also has an outstanding display of fruits. The crab-apples are produced in abundance and are bright yellow, remaining on the tree until the New Year. The spring blossom is white. This small tree (ultimately 4 metres) is also useful as a Universal Pollinator, able to pollinate any domestic apple tree.

One of the most prolific flowering Crab-Apples is *Malus floribunda*, the Japanese Crab. The branches are covered in crimson buds in mid spring that open to white flowers flushed with pink. Once the flowers are over, small inedible yellow fruits appear on the branches amid the fresh green leaves. The tree is attractive in habit, having a rounded crown almost as broad as it is tall (ultimately 7 metres).

~ Hazel ~

Corylus avellana

These lovely trees are grown for their leaf shape and colour, the early spring catkins and the edible nuts in autumn. They are easy to grow and tolerate shade as well as poor soil conditions.

The common Hazel or cobnut is native to Europe. It is a rounded, multi-stemmed shrub with a spreading habit and is useful for hedging.

The Hazel is believed to have magical powers and it is still popular with water diviners who use a forked branch to locate water. Traditionally, the divining rod should be cut on St John's Eve or night (23rd/24th June). Up until the sixteenth century the Hazel rod was also used to detect thieves. Just as when used for water divining, the rod supposedly twitched vigorously when carried towards villains.

The Hazel has many other uses in country lore. A cow's milk yield would be increased if she ate hazel leaves. A double hazelnut carried in the pocket would prevent toothache, and adder bites could be healed by laying hazel twigs across the wound in the shape of a cross.

The cultivated varieties of Hazel are divided into those that carry an abundance of nuts and those that are more ornamental. 'Contorta' is grown mainly for its corkscrew-like stems and branches, an elegant sight when sparkling with frost. 'Aurea' has leaves that flush pale yellow, gradually becoming greener in late summer. Both these varieties are slow growing, reaching a maximum height of 3 metres. *Corylus maxima* 'Kentish Cob' is grown mainly for its nuts and is most attractive when grown as a multi-stemmed shrub rather than as a single-stemmed tree. It will achieve a height of 6 metres.

One of Cicely Mary Barker's first Flower Fairy paintings was the Hazel-Catkin Fairy who now appears in *Flower Fairies of the Winter*.

The White Bryony Fairy

~ THE SONG of ~
THE WHITE BRYONY FAIRY

Have you seen at Autumn-time
Fairy-folk adorning
All the hedge with necklaces,
Early in the morning?
Green beads and red beads
Threaded on a vine:
Is there any handiwork
Prettier than mine?

*(This Bryony has other names—White Vine, Wild Vine, and
Red-berried Bryony. It has tendrils to climb with, which Black Bryony
has not, and its leaves and berries are quite different.
They say its root is white, as the other's is black.)*

~ The Song of ~
The Beechnut Fairy

O the great and happy Beech,
   Glorious and tall!
Changing with the changing months,
   Lovely in them all:

Lovely in the leafless time,
   Lovelier in green;
Loveliest with golden leaves
   And the sky between,

When the nuts are falling fast,
   Thrown by little me—
Tiny things to patter down
   From a forest tree!

(You may eat these.)

The Beechnut Fairy

~ White Bryony ~
Bryonia cretica

This twining plant is common in hedgerows and woodland margins throughout the south of England. The stems climb by means of simple tendrils, which arise from the side of the deciduous, triangular, hairy leaves. The male and female flowers are borne on separate plants, with the male blossom being nearly twice as large. The berries are greenish-white, turning red and then black when fully ripe, and they make a spectacular display in the autumn. However, they are poisonous to humans.

Cicely tells us that tradition has it that White Bryony's roots are white, as Black Bryony's are black. They are in fact light yellow.

~ Beech ~
Fagus sylvatica

As Cicely indicates in her rhyme, the Beech is one of the most attractive native trees. Its elegant shape, fresh foliage and glorious autumn colours give it appeal all year round. Cicely drew the Beech Tree

Fairy in springtime for *Flower Fairies of the Trees*. If left to grow unchecked the Beech tree will grow more than 30 metres high, yet it can be grown as a hedging plant since clipping does not harm the tree in any way. If clipped in mid-summer the leaves stay on the branches, giving the added bonus of a russet covering through the winter. It is one of the best large trees for chalky soils.

Beech woods cover much of the North Downs in the south of England, and these are a spectacular sight in autumn, the colours covering all shades of yellow, copper, gold and bronze. The Beechnuts are enclosed in a hard prickly husk and are a joy for children to gather, revealing the dark brown shiny nut inside. Older beech trees sometimes arch their lower branches to the ground, and this again makes the trees a wonderful haunt for children.

None of the cultivars of the Beech are suitable for anything other than a large garden, but there is a surprising variety of colours and shapes available. *Fagus sylvatica* 'Dawyck Gold' has particularly striking leaves, opening bright yellow and gradually changing to a pale yellow by the summer. 'Dawyck Purple' has rich deep purple leaves throughout the season. Both varieties have a conical, upright habit and ultimately make slightly smaller trees than their parent. 'Pendula' is a beautiful weeping form of the common Beech, with curtains of green leaves on its trailing branches. It may eventually reach 18 metres in height, with a spread of 10 metres.

The Hawthorn Fairy

192

~ The Song of ~
The Hawthorn Fairy

These thorny branches bore the May
　　So many months ago,
That when the scattered petals lay
　　Like drifts of fallen snow,
　　"This is the story's end," you said;
　　But O, not half was told!
For see, my haws are here instead,
And hungry birdies shall be fed
　　On these when days are cold.

~ The Song of ~
The Privet Fairy

Here in the wayside hedge I stand,
And look across the open land;
Rejoicing thus, unclipped and free,
I think how you must envy me,
O garden Privet, prim and neat,
With tidy gravel at your feet!

*(In early summer the Privet has spikes of
very strongly-scented white flowers.)*

194

The Privet Fairy

The Sloe Fairy

196

~ The Song of ~
The Sloe Fairy

When Blackthorn blossoms leap to sight,
They deck the hedge with starry light,
 In early Spring
 When rough winds blow,
 Each promising
 A purple sloe.

And now is Autumn here, and lo,
The Blackthorn bears the purple sloe!
 But ah, how much
 Too sharp these plums,
 Until the touch
 Of Winter comes!

*(The sloe is a wild plum. One bite will set your
teeth on edge until it has been mellowed by frost;
but it is not poisonous.)*

197

~ Hawthorn ~

Crataegus monogyna

Hawthorn's common name is May, the month in which it displays its wonderful creamy-white blossom. It is a shrub or small tree with light grey bark, thorny twigs and toothed dark green leaves. The spring blossom is followed by abundant shiny red fruits. Hawthorn is very common in all parts of Britain other than the most northern parts of Scotland. It is happy in hedgerows and thickets or standing alone, and tolerates stony, shallow soil, as well as drought. It is a very useful hedging plant.

Folklore tells us that Hawthorn blossom should not be brought into the house. Anyone who does so is bringing bad luck or sickness into the family. Simply sitting under the tree is believed to be dangerous in Cornwall, as the pixies who live in the tree will take you into their power. However, in the Cotswolds, Hawthorn is believed to protect you from evil spirits and spells, and branches of May should be tied to the outside of houses, stables and barns in order to repel the pixies coming to steal the milk and to provide protection against witches.

The pagan 'Green Man' symbol of fertility wears a Hawthorn wreath, and this can still be seen in some Medieval church carvings.

The Glastonbury Thorn is a Hawthorn tree that is believed to have sprung from a staff carried by St Joseph of Arimethea. Joseph was a follower of Jesus who offered his tomb for Jesus's body. Legend has it that Joseph of Arimethea went to Britain to convert the barbarians, taking with him the Roman spear that had pierced Christ's side and the Holy

Grail that had been used at the last supper. Some of the old tales say that Christ accompanied him. William Blake's famous hymn 'Jerusalem' refers to this story: 'And did those feet in ancient time/Walk upon England's mountains green?' Joseph of Arimethea's story became inextricably linked with that of King Arthur, and one of the tales tells how Joseph stuck his staff into the side of Glastonbury hill and it burst into flower, creating the Glastonbury Thorn.

The garden variety traditionally believed to be the Glastonbury Thorn is 'Biflora', which occasionally produces an extra crop of flowers in winter and comes into leaf earlier than other Hawthorns. Perhaps for this reason the Glastonbury Thorn was popularly believed to burst into flower at midnight on Christmas Eve.

Crataegus laevigata or Midland Thorn is another British native. The showy white flowers, flushed with pink, appear in late spring, followed by red berries. It will reach a height of 5 metres. 'Paul's Scarlet' is a particularly striking variety, bearing double red flowers in spring. These stand out superbly from the deep green foliage. However, it does not produce many berries.

Cicely Mary Barker painted the May Fairy with her white blossom for *Flower Fairies of the Spring*.

~ Privet ~

Ligustrum vulgare

Wild Privet is commonly found in hedges and thickets in England and Wales. It has shiny mid-green leaves and bears small upright candles of white flowers in June and July. The flowers have an unpleasant smell. The berries appear in late summer and are small, shiny and black. They are attractive to birds.

The garden varieties of Privet include *L. Japonicum* (japanese privet). This large evergreen shrub can be used as a hedging plant or as a single specimen. It has glossy, deep green, oval leaves and bears upright flower clusters in mid summer and early autumn. Its ultimate height is 3.5 metres.

~ Sloe ~

Prunus spinosa

Sloe is the fruit of the Blackthorn, a very hardy native shrub whose spiky twigs and black bark give it its name. It is common throughout Britain and is a charming sight in early spring when it is covered in a dazzling display of white flowers. Cicely painted the Blackthorn Fairy in March with her 'starry blossoms'.

The small blue-black sloes are borne in the autumn and are very sour to taste. However, sloe gin is still popular in country areas.

There are many superstitions attached to Blackthorn. Like May blossom, Blackthorn threatens disaster if brought into the house. It has a reputation for being an omen of death, and was once believed to be the tree from which Christ's crown of thorns was made. Like the Glastonbury Thorn (see Hawthorn), Blackthorn is said to bloom at midnight on Christmas Eve. As a result, some West Country people used it in Christmas decorations, but only when it had first been scorched by fire. This probably derives from its past use in pagan fire festivals, and echoes of this can be found in areas where branches of Blackthorn are burned and the ashes scattered to ensure fertility for the next year's crops.

There are two garden varieties of *Prunus spinosa*, both of which are grown for their spring blossom. 'Purpurea' has purple leaves that fade to pale green, while 'Plena' has double flowers. They are relatively slow growing and will achieve a height of 3 metres in ten years.

Blackthorn's closest domestic-fruit bearing relative is the plum, *Prunus domestica*. Two varieties are particularly reliable: 'Denniston's Superb' and 'Oullin's Gage'. Both are self-fertile and show an abundance of blossom, usually followed by a good crop of fruit.

~ AUTUMN FEASTS and TRADITIONS ~

Probably the best known Autumn tradition today is that of Hallowe'en. In the Christian calendar, All Hallows' Eve (31 October) is the first in the three-day cycle of Hallow Tide, followed by All Hallows' Day (1 November) and All Saints' Day (2 November). It is a period of reflection, remembering those who have died, and marking the end of the old year, looking forward to Christmas. It is also a time to celebrate the harvest, and of course, until relatively recently, to slaughter enough livestock to ensure survival through the winter months.

There are many who feel that the Christian festival has been debased recently, with children dressing up as ghosts and witches and demanding 'Trick or treat?' when knocking on neighbours' doors. It is interesting to note that if we look at the pagan customs that were incorporated into the present religious festivals, we find that the children are celebrating in a manner that would have been quite familiar two thousand years ago.

To the Celts the end of October marked the ending of one year and the beginning of another. It was the time to finish planting the seeds for next year's crops, looking to the future, and also a time to celebrate the successful completion of that year's harvest. The Celts marked the coming of their New Year with the fire festival of Samhain, celebrated around the time of Hallowe'en. Sacred bonfires were lit, the priests put on special robes, and ritual dances were performed. Certain animals were sacrificed to their gods, and some of the livestock was slaughtered in order to be salted down and stored for the winter. The feast was one of purification and the fires were thought to banish evil powers.

To celebrate the harvest, Celts would bring gifts of food to their gods, often going from door to door in order to collect the offerings. The priests would also expect every family to donate kindling and firewood for the bonfire. Could this be the origin of 'Trick or treat?'

After the feasting it was the custom to take home an ember from the bonfire and re-light the fire in the family hearth. The ember was usually carried in a holder – often a turnip or gourd, and in order to scare off evil spirits this was carved to resemble a scary face. These days it is more usual to use a carved pumpkin to hold the 'ember'! The Celts would also dress up to confuse any evil spirits, and this is reflected in the many costumes today.

In Britain, although the Celts declined, the feasts and fires continued. For the three days that had marked Samhain the accustomed order was turned upside down. Men dressed as women, fools dressed as kings, stock was moved into different fields, fences were broken and gates removed. Children knocked on doors asking for food and treats. These traditions continued until the rise of Cromwell and the puritans. Hallowe'en and indeed all the great feast days were then discouraged, though many country areas continued their festivals, albeit on a smaller scale.

The Victorians saw a resurgence of interest in Hallowe'en, with many old customs such as apple-bobbing, roasting chestnuts on street fires and spiced ale enjoying a comeback.

The feasts of harvest time and the looking forward to next year's crops have been at the heart of man's celebrations for millennia, and though Cicely Mary Barker would undoubtedly have had reservations about the pagan elements within the traditions, she would have been the first to join in a thanksgiving for the crops and plants that she herself so valued.

~ABOUT~
FLOWER FAIRIES OF THE WINTER

Cicely Mary Barker published seven collections of Flower Fairy paintings—for *Spring*, *Summer*, *Autumn*, the *Garden*, the *Wayside*, *Trees* and a *Flower Fairy Alphabet*. In 1985, twelve years after her death, her then publisher Blackie reissued the whole series and decided to change the arrangement. By extracting appropriate Flower Fairies from the seven existing books, they were able to compile a volume of *Flower Fairies of the Winter*. This new set of eight titles, which now included a Flower Fairies book for every season of the year, proved extremely popular and the books have continued to be published in this way ever since.

A large number of the Winter Flower Fairies originally appeared as Flower Fairies of the Autumn, but Snowdrop, Dead-Nettle, Shepherd's Purse, Groundsel and Hazel-Catkin were Spring fairies, Winter Jasmine and Winter Aconite were Garden fairies, the Plane, Pine, Box, Blackthorn and Christmas Tree Fairies were fairies of the Trees, and the Rush-Grass, Cotton-Grass and Totter-Grass Fairies came from the Wayside. Now they are firmly established together as a collection that honours the plants and flowers that flourish in what Cicely Mary Barker called 'the grey of the year'.

FLOWER FAIRIES
of the WINTER

The Snowdrop Fairy

~ The Song of ~
The Snowdrop Fairy

Deep sleeps the Winter,
    Cold, wet, and grey;
Surely all the world is dead;
    Spring is far away.
Wait! the world shall waken;
    It is not dead, for lo,
The Fair Maids of February
    Stand in the snow!

~ The Song of ~
The Yew Fairy

Here, on the dark and solemn Yew,
　　A marvel may be seen,
Where waxen berries, pink and new,
　　Appear amid the green.

I sit a-dreaming in the tree,
　　So old and yet so new;
One hundred years, or two, or three
　　Are little to the Yew.

I think of bygone centuries,
　　And seem to see anew
The archers face their enemies
　　With bended bows of Yew.

The Yew Fairy

~ Snowdrop ~

Galanthus nivalis

There are few sights more welcome in the bleak days of winter than the delicate white bell of the Snowdrop. Said to resemble an angel on a snowflake, the dainty flowers give assurance that spring will come. Traditionally, the Snowdrop symbolises hope and purity. On the Feast of the Purification (2 February), it was a medieval custom for virgins, dressed in white, to bring posies of Snowdrops into church and strew them on the altar. This explains the Snowdrop's country name of 'fair maids of February', alluded to in the rhyme.

The Snowdrop is native to Britain and can still be seen growing wild in open woodland and hedgerows. It is a very popular garden plant and will spread to form patches beneath shrubs and trees, as well as naturalising easily in grass. Whether planted in drifts or in small groups to draw the eye, there is no doubting its impact on the winter garden. One of the most popular and reliable garden varieties is 'Flore Pleno', also known as the Double Snowdrop. It has many-petalled white flowers with green markings, and strong strap-shaped leaves. A taller Snowdrop variety is *Galanthus caucasicus*, which grows to about 25 centimetres, more than twice as high as its cousins. This striking Snowdrop has broad blue-green leaves and single pure-white flowers. All Snowdrops prefer moist soils.

Many gardeners find that Snowdrops can be difficult to grow from dry bulbs. It is possible to buy Snowdrops 'in the green', with leaves and flowers, and to plant them in the spring. They will usually establish themselves more easily.

~ *Yew* ~

Taxus baccata

The Yew played an important part in British history. As Cicely Mary Barker mentions in her rhyme, the long bows in the Middle Ages were made of Yew, which is very strong yet flexible. This gave the archers a much greater firing range than with bows made of lesser wood. Yew trees are long-lived but very slow growing, and in order to meet the demand for the wood, more Yews were planted. This caused some difficulty as all parts of the tree are poisonous to people and livestock and it should not be planted in fields or pasture. Some say this is the reason so many Yews were planted in churchyards.

The Yew's history goes back even further. The Druids held it sacred and used it in their religious rituals, planting it at their sacred sites. Yew trees continue to hold a fascination for us today. Some Yews in England are said to have been old when William the Conqueror landed. Perhaps because of its association with consecrated ground, it is believed to keep witches away. It symbolises sorrow.

The poison it contains, taxine, is now used in medicine.

The evergreen Yew is popular for garden hedging, though children must be warned that it is poisonous. Regular clipping eliminates the berries and encourages dense growth that is ideally suited to topiary. It will achieve a height of more than 20 metres if left unchecked. If growing Yew as a tree the variety 'Dovastonii Aurea' is an elegant choice. The golden foliage is held on tiers of horizontal branches. It is non-fruiting and will grow to approximately 5 metres.

The Winter Jasmine Fairy

212

~ The Song of ~
The Winter Jasmine Fairy

All through the Summer my leaves were green,
But never a flower of mine was seen;
Now Summer is gone, that was so gay,
And my little green leaves are shed away.
            In the grey of the year
            What cheer, what cheer?

The Winter is come, the cold winds blow;
I shall feel the frost and the drifting snow;
But the sun can shine in December too,
And this is the time of my gift to you.
            See here, see here,
            My flowers appear!

The swallows have flown beyond the sea,
But friendly Robin, he stays with me;
And little Tom-Tit, so busy and small,
Hops where the jasmine is thick on the wall;
            And we say: "Good cheer!
            We're here! We're here!"

~ The Song of ~
The Dead-Nettle Fairy

Through sun and rain, the country lane,
The field, the road, are my abode.
Though leaf and bud be splashed with mud,
Who cares? Not I!—I see the sky,
The kindly sun, the wayside fun
Of tramping folk who smoke and joke,
The bairns who heed my dusty weed
(No sting have I to make them cry),
And truth to tell, they love me well.
My brothers, White, and Yellow bright,
Are finer chaps than I, perhaps;
Who cares? Not I! So now good-bye.

The Dead-Nettle Fairy

The Rush-Grass and Cotton-Grass Fairies

216

~ THE SONG of ~
THE RUSH-GRASS AND
COTTON-GRASS FAIRIES

Safe across the moorland
    Travellers may go,
If they heed our warning—
    We're the ones who know!

Let the footpath guide you—
    You'll be safely led;
There is bog beside you
    Where you cannot tread!

Mind where you are going!
    If you turn aside
Where you see us growing,
    Trouble will betide.

Keep you to the path, then!
    Hark to what we say!
Else, into the quagmire
    You will surely stray.

~ *Winter Jasmine* ~
Jasminum nudiflorum

This deciduous, winter-flowering shrub is not native to Britain but is now naturalised in many areas. It is a very rewarding plant, tolerant of all aspects and soil conditions, from a dry sunny site to deep shade, as long as its roots are not waterlogged. Deservedly popular, it flowers reliably year after year, its long slender shoots bearing cheerful yellow flowers through the winter and well into the spring.

~ *Dead-Nettle* ~
Lamium purpureum

The rather off-putting name of this plant refers to its close resemblance to the stinging nettle, but without the stinging hairs. It is very common in Britain and can be seen in fields, wasteland, roadsides and gardens.

The 'brothers, White, and Yellow bright' referred to in the rhyme are the White Dead-nettle *Lamium album* and the Yellow Archangel *Lamiastrum galeobdolon*.

~ Rush-Grass and Cotton-Grass ~

Juncus squarrosus and *Eriophorum angustifolium*

The Heath Rush is a native perennial, forming dense tufts easily recognized by the straight, tough flowering stem in the centre. It is common on acid soils on moorland heaths and bogs, especially where sheep grazing is heavy. It will grow up to half a metre in height.

The most attractive native rush grass is the Flowering Rush, *Butomus umbellatus*. This has been used in ornamental water gardens for centuries. Grown for its twisted, rush-like leaves and loose clusters of pale pink flowers, it is happiest when planted in full sun in any fertile soil in water up to 25 centimetres deep.

Rushes, with their strong but supple leaves have been used for weaving baskets from ancient times, and have thus earned the meaning of docility.

Cotton-grass is a member of the Sedge family of flowering grasses. The plants belonging to this family have characteristically triangular stems and are common in wet, marshy areas of Britain. They have an ecological importance because their root systems help to bind and stabilize soils. Cotton-grass is easily recognised by the creamy seedheads that look like tufts of cotton wool.

The stems and leaves of many of the Sedge grasses are used for weaving and papermaking. Most importantly, specific varieties of Cotton-grass grown in North America became the basis for the cotton industry that was a major part of the British Industrial Revolution.

The Spindle Berry Fairy

~ The Song of ~
The Spindle Berry Fairy

See the rosy-berried Spindle
All to sunset colours turning,
Till the thicket seems to kindle,
Just as though the trees were burning.
While my berries split and show
Orange-coloured seeds aglow,
One by one my leaves must fall:
Soon the wind will take them all.
Soon must fairies shut their eyes
For the Winter's hushabies;
But, before the Autumn goes,
Spindle turns to flame and rose!

~ THE SONG of ~
THE SHEPHERD'S PURSE FAIRY

Though I'm poor to human eyes
Really I am rich and wise.
Every tiny flower I shed
Leaves a heart-shaped purse instead.

In each purse is wealth indeed—
Every coin a living seed.
Sow the seed upon the earth—
Living plants shall spring to birth.

Silly people's purses hold
Lifeless silver, clinking gold;
But you cannot grow a pound
From a farthing in the ground.

Money may become a curse:
Give me then my Shepherd's Purse.

The Shepherd's Purse Fairy

The Groundsel Fairy

~ The Song of ~
The Groundsel Fairy

If dicky-birds should buy and sell
In tiny markets, I can tell
    The way they'd spend their money.
They'd ask the price of cherries sweet,
They'd choose the pinkest worms for meat,
And common Groundsel for a treat,
    Though you might think it funny.

Love me not, or love me well;
That's the way they'd buy and sell.

225

~ Spindle Berry ~

Euonymus europaeus

The Spindle Berry is common in hedgerows throughout Britain, especially on chalky or sandy soils. The flowers are generally inconspicuous, but as Cicely tells us in her rhyme, the leaves colour to a deep red in autumn, a show enhanced by the bright red or pink fruit. Most of the species are native to Europe. The wood from the Spindle Berry was once commonly used for carving. Later, as other more exotic woods replaced it, it was primarily used to make spindles – hence its name.

Many species of Euonymus are cultivated. The deciduous species such as *Euonymus alatus* are grown for their eye-catching autumn foliage and distinctive lobed fruit.

~ Shepherd's Purse ~

Capsella bursa-pastoris

As Cicely Mary Barker's rhyme suggests, this plant's attractive name comes from the purse-shaped seed-pod left after the flowers have fallen. Shepherd's Purse grows well on rich grassland and along embankments, and is common throughout Britain. It is a member of the

Mustard family and, like its cousins the Hedge Mustard and Winter-cress, prefers soil that is neither too wet nor too dry and is very rich in nutrients. Shepherd's Purse has a robust, earthy smell, which can be unpleasant after rain.

～ Groundsel ～

Senecio vulgaris

Groundsel is very common throughout Britain. It is found in gardens, fields and grasslands, particularly near ponds and ditches, as it prefers a damp site. After flowering the small white hairy fruits look a little like the white hair of an old man, and this is reflected in the Latin name Senecio, from senex – old man. As Cicely tells us in her rhyme, Groundsel is a popular treat for canaries and other birds.

Groundsel's most common garden relatives are asters, which bring welcome colour to the garden in late summer and autumn.

The autumn-flowering asters are known as Michaelmas daisies because they flower around Michaelmas (29 September), named after the church festival held in honour of St Michael, the archangel. These hardy perennials make a fine show in the border, particularly when planted in large single-coloured groups. Asters suffered a decline in popularity in recent years because of a perceived tendency to mildew. However, certain varieties have been bred to be mildew resistant. These include the *Aster x frikartii* cultivars and *Aster novae-angliae* 'Herbstschnee' (white) and 'Andenken an Alma Potschke' (cerise). The *Aster novae-angliae* cultivars require little staking.

The Lords-and-Ladies Fairy

228

~ The Song of ~
The Lords-and-Ladies Fairy

Fairies, when you lose your way,
　　From the dance returning,
In the darkest undergrowth
　　See my candles burning!
These shall make the pathway plain
Homeward to your beds again.

*(These are the berries of the Wild Arum, which has many
other names, and has a flower like a hood in the Spring.
The berries are not to be eaten.)*

~ The Song of ~
The Plane Tree Fairy

You will not find him in the wood,
    Nor in the country lane;
But in the city's parks and streets
    You'll see the Plane.

O turn your eyes from pavements grey,
    And look you up instead,
To where the Plane tree's pretty balls
    Hang overhead!

When he has shed his golden leaves,
    His balls will yet remain,
To deck the tree until the Spring
    Comes back again!

The Plane Tree Fairy

~ Lords-and-Ladies ~

Arum maculatum

Lords-and-Ladies are common in England and Wales, though rarer in Scotland because of their preference for warm situations. They enjoy loose, loamy soil, rich in nutrients, and are often found in woodland glades and along hedgerows. The flowers have an unmistakable hooded shape. Cicely Mary Barker drew Lords-and-Ladies in flower in *Flower Fairies of the Spring.* The colour of the pointed 'spadix' held within the hood can vary from white to violet, and it emits a rather unpleasant odour of decay in order to attract flies and other pollinating insects. In late summer the leaves and hood die back and are replaced with bright red berries.

All Arum berries are poisonous and the plant sap and berry juice can cause skin irritation.

232

~ Plane Tree ~

Platanus

'In the city's parks and streets\You'll see the Plane.' As Cicely Mary Barker's rhyme suggests, Plane Trees are a familiar feature of our cities. They are tolerant of atmospheric pollution and are therefore widely planted in urban areas. The variety *Platanus x hispanica* is known as the London Plane because it is so common in that city. Plane Trees are less suitable for garden planting because of their enormous size (ultimately 45 metres) and the dense shade cast by their spreading branches. However, if given sufficient room, the distinctively mottled bark, strings of bristly fruits and glossy green leaves make the Plane Tree a handsome choice. Vigorous and uncomplicated, the Plane will grow in sun or shade in any soil.

The Plane Tree was popular in Ancient times. In Athens there was a long avenue of Plane Trees that became a meeting-place for Greek philosophers. Many hours were spent pacing up and down beneath the spreading branches whilst engaged in heated philosophical discussions. As a result, the Plane Tree was appointed the emblem of genius.

Folklore credits the Plane with medicinal virtues too. To heal general ills, simply chew the bark taken straight from the trunk. If taken for a cold, the bark should be boiled first.

The Burdock Fairy

234

~ The Song of ~
The Burdock Fairy

Wee little hooks on each brown little bur,
(Mind where you're going, O Madam and Sir!)
How they will cling to your skirt-hem and stocking!
Hear how the Burdock is laughing and mocking:
Try to get rid of me, try as you will,
Shake me and scold me, I'll stick to you still,
      I'll stick to you still!

~ The Song of ~
The Pine Tree Fairy

A tall, tall tree is the Pine tree,
　　With its trunk of bright red-brown—
The red of the merry squirrels
　　Who go scampering up and down.

There are cones on the tall, tall Pine tree,
　　With its needles sharp and green;
Small seeds in the cones are hidden,
　　And they ripen there unseen.

The elves play games with the squirrels
　　At the top of the tall, tall tree,
Throwing cones for the squirrels to nibble—
　　I wish I were there to see!

The Pine Tree Fairy

237

The Holly Fairy

~ The Song of ~
The Holly Fairy

O, I am green in Winter-time,
   When other trees are brown;
Of all the trees (So saith the rhyme)
   The holly bears the crown.
December days are drawing near
   When I shall come to town,
And carol-boys go singing clear
Of all the trees (O hush and hear!)
   The holly bears the crown!

For who so well-beloved and merry
As the scarlet Holly Berry?

~ Burdock ~
Arctium minus

Burdock is scattered throughout Britain. Most commonly found alongside paths and on wasteland, the plant will only grow where the soil is rich in nitrogen. Burdock flowers in mid to late summer, its purple thistle-like florets carried on erect branches. The leaves are large and slightly heart-shaped. The bracts are hooked and will cling to clothing or hair, enabling the plant to scatter its seeds over a wide area. This tenacity has made Burdock the symbol for importunity. The plant also carries the meaning 'touch me not', warning passers-by against becoming inextricably tangled with its burs. Burdock roots were once used to make a pain-relieving drink for women in labour.

~ Pine Tree ~
Pinus sylvestris

The Scots Pine is the only true British native pine. It is fast-growing when young but slows down with age, developing a flattened crown above a tall trunk which can be over 20 metres tall before the branches begin. The pine-cones are egg-shaped, ripening from green to brown and crack open in late summer to scatter the seeds. The cones themselves fall in large quantities in both autumn and spring. The Scots Pine will grow to more than 35 metres in height and is only suitable for the larger garden. However, some of its garden varieties have been bred to a smaller size.

~ Holly ~

Ilex aquifolium

The native Holly is common throughout Britain, found in deciduous and coniferous woods on all but very wet soils. It is very shade-tolerant, has shiny evergreen leaves and bears bright red berries from autumn through the depths of winter. Its blossom is usually white but insignificant. All holly berries are attractive to birds and sustain them when other foods are scarce. Surprisingly, Holly will grow up to 20 metres tall if left unchecked, making a conical tree.

Like the Yew, Holly was an important part of the Druids' religion. Its popularity has continued through the centuries, although its significance has changed. Decorating the house at Yuletide with branches of Holly and berries delighted the fairies and so brought good fortune. This tradition is still adhered to in many homes, though now it is considered part of the Christmas festival. The association between the Holly and the Ivy was a central part of the pagan religion. Holly, with its bright red berries, was seen as a symbol of the feminine aspect. Ivy was seen to represent the masculine. The ancient custom of decorating doorways with the plants intertwined was a symbolic union of the two.

The Box-Tree Fairy

~ THE SONG of ~
THE BOX-TREE FAIRY

Have you seen the Box unclipped,
Never shaped and never snipped?
Often it's a garden hedge,
Just a narrow little edge;
Or in funny shapes it's cut,
And it's very pretty; but—

But, unclipped, it is a tree,
Growing as it likes to be;
And it has its blossoms too;
Tiny buds, the Winter through,
Wait to open in the Spring
In a scented yellow ring.

And among its leaves there play
Little blue-tits, brisk and gay.

~ The Song of ~
The Old-Man's Beard Fairy

This is where the little elves
Cuddle down to hide themselves;
Into fluffy beds they creep,
Say good-night, and go to sleep.

*(Old-Man's Beard is Wild Clematis; its flowers are called
Traveller's Joy. This silky fluff belongs to the seeds.)*

The Old-Man's Beard Fairy

~ Box Tree ~

Buxus sempervirens

The Box Tree is found throughout Britain but is particularly abundant in southern England. It is a slow-growing evergreen shrub that prefers chalk or limestone soils and can be found in sunny, open locations as well as shady beech woods. If left unchecked as Cicely Mary Barker's rhyme suggests, it can achieve the height of a small tree. It flowers in mid to late spring, carrying small yellow blossoms in clusters where the leaf joins the stem.

Unaffected by the changing of the seasons, its enduring qualities have made Box ideal for use in topiary, and it has become the symbol of stoicism.

Dwarf hedges used in parterres are traditionally composed of Box. The deep green glossy foliage contrasts well with bright flowers and gravel paths. The smaller cultivars can be easily grown in pots and are useful for a formal design. The garden varieties include 'Elegantissima'. a compact bush with variegated cream and green leaves, and 'Suffruticosa', a small shrub traditonally used for edging flowerbeds. The leaves are very dense and can be clipped hard every year.

~ Old-Man's Beard Fairy ~

Clematis vitalba

The feathery white seedheads of Old-Man's Beard scrambling through hedgerows and thickets are a common sight in winter. They are the fruits of the native wild clematis, which is common throughout southern England and Wales. It is seldom found further north than South Yorkshire because of its preference for warmth and it has colonised only moderately hilly areas.

The clematis has a woody climbing stem with heart-shaped leaves. Its flowers are made up of creamy, petal-like sepals, and its sweet fragrance makes its other common name, Traveller's Joy, very well deserved. Cicely Mary Barker included Traveller's Joy in *Flower Fairies of the Summer*.

The juice of the wild clematis can sting the skin and beggars used it to cause ugly sores on their skin and so evoke greater pity from passers-by. This led to it becoming the emblem of artifice and deception.

There are several different types of clematis that flower happily in the garden. Probably the best-known varieties are the large-flowered hybrids, which bloom mainly in the summer. These are available in many colours and will scramble happily over shrubs or up walls and fences. They seldom grow more than 3 metres high.

The Blackthorn Fairy

~ The Song of ~
The Blackthorn Fairy

The wind is cold, the Spring seems long
   a-waking;
    The woods are brown and bare;
Yet this is March: soon April will be making
    All things most sweet and fair.

See, even now, in hedge and thicket tangled,
    One brave and cheering sight:
The leafless branches of the Blackthorn,
    spangled
    With starry blossoms white!

(The cold days of March are sometimes called
Blackthorn Winter".)

~ The Song of ~
The Hazel-Catkin Fairy

Like little tails of little lambs,
    On leafless twigs my catkins swing;
They dingle-dangle merrily
    Before the wakening of Spring.

Beside the pollen-laden tails
    My tiny crimson tufts you see
The promise of the autumn nuts
    Upon the slender hazel tree.

While yet the woods lie grey and still
    I give my tidings: "Spring is near!"
One day the land shall leap to life
    With fairies calling: "Spring is HERE!"

The Hazel-Catkin Fairy

~ Blackthorn ~
Prunus spinosa

The black bark and thorny twigs of this hardy native shrub make it easily identifiable. The white blossom appears before the leaves, and the twigs and flowers make a striking contrast. Blackthorn is common in hedgerows and along verges throughout Britain. In the autumn it bears blue-black, sour sloe berries, which give it its other common name, Sloe. The berries can be used to make the very potent 'Sloe gin'. Cicely drew the Sloe Fairy in *Flower Fairies of the Autumn*.

The blossom first appears in March, often coinciding with a sharp spell of frost. As Cicely tells us, country people call this time 'Blackthorn winter'. Blackthorn's sharp spines are notoriously difficult to untangle from the clothes on which they cling and it has therefore become the emblem for difficulty. However, its persistent flowering through the cold days has also given it a happier significance; that of constancy.

Blackthorn has many garden relatives, all of which bear wonderful spring blossom.

~ Hazel-Catkin ~

Corylus avellana

The Hazel tree, with its pretty yellow catkins in spring and hazelnuts in the autumn is a striking small tree found throughout Britain. According to ancient lore, the little hazelnut embodied knowledge, wisdom and fertility. One Celtic legend tells how a Hazel tree dropped its nuts into a well below it. A salmon swimming in the well ate the hazelnuts. Fionn, a Celtic hero, caught the salmon and cooked it. While he was eating the salmon Fionn tasted one of the nuts it had swallowed and instantly gained all knowledge. For this reason, the hazelnut symbolized wisdom. Cicely has a Hazel-Nut Fairy in *Flower Fairies of the Autumn*.

The Hazel is said to be a lucky tree. A cap of Hazel leaves and twigs ensures safety at sea, while a sprig of Hazel will protect from lightning. Water diviners use Hazel wands to search for hidden springs. For more general use the Hazel's flexibility makes it ideal as an alternative to willow and wicker in baskets and garden decorations.

The Totter-Grass Fairy

~ The Song of ~
The Totter-Grass Fairy

The leaves on the tree-tops
    Dance in the breeze;
Totter-grass dances
    And sways like the trees—

Shaking and quaking!
    While through it there goes,
Dancing, a Fairy,
    On lightest of toes.

(Totter-grass is also called Quaking-grass.)

255

~ The Song of ~
The Winter Aconite Fairy

Deep in the earth
I woke, I stirred.
I said: "Was that the Spring I heard?
For something called!"
"No, no," they said;
"Go back to sleep. Go back to bed.

"You're far too soon;
The world's too cold
For you, so small." So I was told.
But how could I
Go back to sleep?
I could not wait; I had to peep!

Up, up, I climbed,
And here am I.
How wide the earth! How great the sky!
O wintry world,
See me, awake!
Spring calls, and comes; 'tis no mistake.

The Winter Aconite Fairy

~ Totter-Grass ~

Briza media

This native perennial is found throughout the British Isles on most types of grassland, though most common on the chalky ground of southern England. It is tolerant of heavy and poorly drained soils. Totter-grass has little value for grazing as it produces very few leaves. However, the dangling heart-shaped flower heads shaking in the breeze make it one of the most attractive grasses, and it is often dried and used for winter flower arrangements. The variety 'Limouzi' has larger flower-heads and grey-green leaves.

Cicely also includes Totter-grass's other name, Quaking-grass.

Grasses are an often under-used feature in the garden. For many people, grass means the lawn. However, many grasses make effective specimen plants and look attractive in borders, their feathery foliage and flowers bringing movement into the garden as they sway in the breeze. A great bonus is that grasses need little attention and yet have a long season of interest. What they lack in colour they more than make up for with their sculptural leaves and flowerheads.

The true grass family, the *Gramineae*, includes the bamboo and pampas grasses. Bamboos are an essential element in a Japanese style garden. They make good screens and their dramatic combination of tall canes and rustling evergreen foliage also makes them a splendid focal point. The flowerheads, produced in mid summer, are a dull brown and can make the bamboo look untidy. However, as plants bloom at irregular intervals, some only every hundred years, this is not a significant problem. Bamboos are generally hardy but prefer a sunny position. When choosing a bamboo variety it is best to check whether they are clump-forming or have running rhizomes which need to be confined lest they take over the garden.

Pampas grass (*Cortaderia selloana*) forms dense clumps of arching, evergreen leaves and tall stems bearing showy silvery plumes up to 45 centimetres long. These are produced in late summer and last into winter.

~ Winter Aconite ~

Eranthis hyemalis

The Winter Aconite is one of the first flowers to bloom in spring, sometimes even before the snowdrop. The cheerful yellow flowers peep out from their ruffs of feathery green leaves and look a little like oversized buttercups. Winter Aconites like well-drained soil and some shade in the summer, so the protection of deciduous shrubs or trees is ideal. The plants grow to about 10 centimetres in height and multiply rapidly, eventually forming a charming floral carpet.

Winter Aconites look at their best when planted in large groups, perhaps naturalized in a shrub border or beneath trees. They associate particularly well with the blue or white stars of *Anemone blanda*. Like snowdrops, Winter Aconites can be a little difficult to establish when planted as dry tubers. Many nurseries sell them 'in the green' to be planted in early spring. When the foliage has faded it can be raked off.

259

The Christmas Tree Fairy

~ The Song of ~
The Christmas Tree Fairy

The little Christmas Tree was born
 And dwelt in open air;
It did not guess how bright a dress
 Some day its boughs would wear;
Brown cones were all, it thought, a tall
 And grown-up Fir would bear.

O little Fir! Your forest home
 Is far and far away;
And here indoors these boughs of yours
 With coloured balls are gay,
With candle-light, and tinsel bright,
 For this is Christmas Day!

A dolly-fairy stands on top,
 Till children sleep; then she
(A live one now!) from bough to bough
 Goes gliding silently.
O magic sight, this joyous night!
 O laden, sparkling tree!

~ Christmas Tree ~
Pinaceae

It is difficult to imagine Christmas without a Christmas tree. The dark green needles of a fir tree decorated with twinkling candles are a common sight, not only in houses but also in shop windows, market squares and even above the heads of the hurrying shoppers. The Christmas Tree is a central part of the Christmas tradition. It is therefore remarkable that the first Christmas tree came to Britain as recently as 1834, when Prince Albert brought a fir tree to Windsor Castle from his native Germany as a present for Queen Victoria. As with most traditions, however, the roots of the decorated festive tree go back for thousands of years. Many cultures saw the evergreens, which remain green even in winter, as a symbol of life even during the dead season. To decorate with evergreen trees and branches was a way of celebrating eternal life.

The Romans celebrated Saturnalia, their winter festival, by decorating evergreen trees with small, shining pieces of metal in honour of Saturn, the god of metalwork and agriculture. In the Middle Ages, a fir tree was decorated with apples and given the name Paradise Tree as part of the feast of Adam and Eve, held on 24 December.

It was Martin Luther, the great German protestant reformer who is believed to have been the first to decorate an indoor Christmas tree. After a midnight walk through a peaceful pine forest, with the bright stars shining above his head, he tried to recreate the experience for his family by bringing a tree into the house and decorating it with candles. The decorated tree grew in popularity in Germany and Austria, and German settlers in eastern Pennsylvania brought the custom to the United States. Since then the tradition has become established throughout the Western world.

Although we speak of a Christmas Tree, there are many different species that are grown for the purpose. The best-selling trees are the Scotch pine, Douglas fir, Noble fir and Norway Spruce. The Norway Spruce was traditionally the species used to decorate British homes. It was native to the British Isles before the last Ice Age and was reintroduced before the 1500s. Nowadays, however, the different species are grown commercially and it is even possible to choose and fell your own.

The fairy on the top of the Christmas Tree is a very British tradition. In the rest of Europe and Scandinavia a star or angel is the preferred ornament. Quite why the fairy is so popular in this country is unknown, but perhaps it reflects the depth of the Faerie tradition which was driven underground by the arrival of Christianity but continued to be observed at sacred sites such as local wells, springs and trees. Nowadays fairies are thought of as harmless and friendly beings, but for centuries fairies were believed to be tricky, fickle, even malevolent, and they had to be placated with offerings. Country people gave them the name 'Little Folk', in the hope that the pleasant name would rub off on the fairies. The ancient Greeks did the same when they called the terrible Furies 'the Kindly Ones'. It is therefore possible that the Christmas Tree fairy is a remnant of a far older, pagan tradition, perhaps associated with the Winter Solstice, or Yule.

THE TRADTIONAL
~ MEANINGS and USES of PLANTS ~

The relationship between the mediaeval peasant and his garden was intensely practical. The small plot of earth surrounding the peasant's house was stocked with basic beans and herbs that could be used for cooking. At that time the only people who had the leisure time available to create anything remotely decorative were the nobility and the monasteries, and even they were more likely to favour a plant with medicinal virtues or a pleasant scent and taste.

It was Henry VIII's dissolution of the Monasteries that led to the first great change in the peasant's garden. Villagers were now cut off from the herbal medicines that had once been supplied by the monks, and so they began to grow their own; most taken from the old monastery gardens. The traditional names have great charm. Comfrey's other names include 'knitbone' and 'boneset', referring to the belief that it would help to knit broken bones. Golden rod's chief use was for staunching blood from wounds. In some cases, science has proved the monks and the peasants right. Garlic was valued as an antiseptic even in ancient times. More recently the antiseptic properties of garlic have been scientifically proven. An even better example is the opium poppy, which has been known as a drug for relieving the pains of cholera and childbirth for at least two thousand years. Today the chief ingredient of some headache pills, codeine, is produced from the poppy's milky juice. The better known medicine taken from the poppy is morphine.

Less scientific, but charming nevertheless, is the ancient Doctrine of Signatures. It was believed that when the devil let loose disease and pestilence on the earth, God gave us the antidotes in plants throughout our countryside; and that each plant was stamped with a characteristic, or Signature, that tells us how to use it. Probably the best known example is lungwort, whose foliage has white spots. These were thought to resemble the lung scars caused by tuberculosis, and the plant was

264

much sought after as a cure. Science has been unable to substantiate that particular belief, but lungwort is still recommended by some herbalists to treat coughs.

Other plants liberated from the monasteries were grown to add savour to the basic vegetables and meat, often rancid, that was the peasants' diet. Borage added flavour to soup and could be used to make a refreshing tonic. In addition, its young leaves and flowers were added to salads. Dill was used to flavour stews and vinegar, as well as making the ideal fish sauce. Fennel was another favourite, particularly for cheese, fish and pickles, while sage became the ideal accompaniment for pork, chicken and veal. Mint was widely used in drinks and as a sauce for meat, and it was also an important ingredient in many of the alcoholic drinks made by the monks (medicinal, of course!). Other herbs helped to mask the dreadful smells that built up in the small, crowded, rush-strewn houses. A few branches of rosemary or lavender might be scattered through the rooms and perhaps sandwiched between stored clothing in trunks or chests. There were also plants used for making dyes, such as golden rod for yellow and irises for black. There were still more plants that were grown purely for their help in warding off evil. When life was so precarious, it is no wonder that people clung to the hope that certain plants might offer protection. Yew, elder and bay trees were planted partly in order to protect the house from witches. Columbine was believed to protect from plague, as was the wood anemone.

To the medieval peasant the plants were useful in all these different ways, yet their beauty was in many ways incidental, a bonus. Gradually, however, as more gardens were planted with herbs and shrubs, neighbours would barter for cuttings, or plants might be given as gifts. Often the housewife would take over the little plot and might interplant the herbs and vegetables with wild plants seen in the hedgerow; primroses, bluebells, violets and foxgloves. As the centuries passed, more plants became available. Workers at the 'big house' might bring back cuttings of roses and peonies. In the late eighteenth century, when the gentry were creating ornamental parks under the influence of Capability Brown, the estate workers brought home many of the plants that had been discarded by their masters. Thus the true cottage garden was born, with all the plants mingled in a glorious riot of colour that has become the hallmark of the traditional English garden.

~ INDEX ~